Paramedics and Pups

Meet the first responders of Southern Sydney!

Best friends Jennifer Roden and Francesca Moretti have dedicated themselves to helping others. Long hours working as paramedics haven't left much time for romance—which suits these friends just fine! Jenny and Frankie each have their own reasons to guard their hearts. But two gorgeous new colleagues and a pair of rescue dogs are about to turn their lives upside down! They might be used to high-pressure rescues, but this time, it's *their* hearts on the line…

Discover how Jenny finds her forever home with small-town doc, and single dad, Dr. Rob Pierson in

Her Off-Limits Single Dad by Marion Lennox

And dive into the roller coaster of Frankie and Nico's relationship in

The Italian, His Pup and Me by Alison Roberts

Both available now!

Dear Reader,

This year the floods that have engulfed Australia's southeast have been horrific. The losses have been appalling, but the rescues and the human kindness truly heartwarming. My heart goes out to all those affected, especially to you, as a reader, if you're suffering personal loss.

As images of these floods fill our nightly news, of course they find their way into my books. This duo, cowritten with the wonderful Alison Roberts, brings in Alison's personal experience as a paramedic, and our heroes and heroines struggle with the perils of their jobs plus the emotional journeys of their growing attractions.

And of course, both Alison and I love dogs. We don't just see them on our nightly news—to quote Edith Wharton, they're a heartbeat at our feet. Which explains the dramas of Stumpy and Bruce.

Enjoy,

Marion Lennox

HER OFF-LIMITS
SINGLE DAD

MARION LENNOX

PAPL
DISCARDED

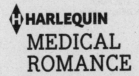

HARLEQUIN

MEDICAL
ROMANCE

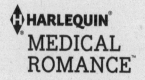

HARLEQUIN®
MEDICAL
ROMANCE™

Recycling programs
for this product may
not exist in your area.

ISBN-13: 978-1-335-59498-3

Her Off-Limits Single Dad

Copyright © 2023 by Marion Lennox

Harlequin Enterprises ULC
22 Adelaide St. West, 41st Floor
Toronto, Ontario M5H 4E3, Canada
www.Harlequin.com

Printed in U.S.A.

Marion Lennox has written over one hundred romance novels and is published in over one hundred countries and thirty languages. Her international awards include the prestigious RITA® Award (twice!) and the *RT Book Reviews* Career Achievement Award for "a body of work which makes us laugh and teaches us about love." Marion adores her family, her kayak, her dog and lying on the beach with a book someone else has written. Heaven!

Books by Marion Lennox

Harlequin Medical Romance

Second Chance with Her Island Doc
Rescued by the Single Dad Doc
Pregnant Midwife on His Doorstep
Mistletoe Kiss with the Heart Doctor
Falling for His Island Nurse
Healing Her Brooding Island Hero
A Rescue Dog to Heal Them
A Family to Save the Doctor's Heart
Dr. Finlay's Courageous Bride
Healed by Their Dolphin Island Baby

Harlequin Romance

Cinderella and the Billionaire

Visit the Author Profile page
at Harlequin.com for more titles.

**Praise for
Marion Lennox**

"What an entertaining, fast-paced, emotionally charged read Ms. Lennox has delivered in this book…. The way this story started had me hooked immediately."
—*Harlequin Junkie* on *The Baby They Longed For*

CHAPTER ONE

THIS SEEMED LIKE a job for Air Rescue. The nearest helicopter base, though, was South Sydney, and their only available unit was caught up on another job.

They were on their own.

The crashed truck, on its side well below the road, seemed to have caught on a straggly coastal gumtree. From where Jenny stood it was a good ten metres down to the truck, then another ten to the rock-strewn surf beneath. The truck seemed to be balanced across the tree trunk. It looked like it could slip further at any minute and there seemed no way they could safely climb down.

'Are we sure someone's inside?' she asked, and Gary grimaced.

'We're pretty sure.'

Jennifer Roden and Gary Drummond, Willhua's only two paramedics, had been called to this crash by Chris, Willhua's sole police officer. Chris, though, was caught up with a break-in and assault. He'd taken the frantic call from a member of the public, but could do nothing but pass the message to the ambulance service. That meant Gary and Jen were first on scene. First things first—they needed to check this wasn't just a vehicle pushed over the cliff to avoid dumping charges.

From where they stood the truck looked old and rusty, and if it was worthless it'd be costly to get rid of. How much cheaper to drive it here, release the parking brakes and give it a push into the sea?

That'd be the easy scenario but it didn't fit here.

'Deirdre McConachie saw it go over.' Gary, Jenny's partner and Willhua's senior paramedic, was staring down at the truck and looking grim. 'Deirdre didn't have her phone—she had to drive into town to call Chris. She told him the truck was weaving all over the road in front of her—she thought the driver might be drunk. She said it went straight down. Going over here... Well, Deirdre assumed it'd ended up in the sea and there'd be no hope of survival. She was too scared to look—she just headed fast into town for help—but by the look of the truck she guessed it might be Charlie Emerson.'

'Who's Charlie?' Jen had only been in this job,

in this town, for two days. Gary had worked here for thirty years and knew everyone.

'Retired farmer. Hell, I'll ring Chris back. We need urgent help. More cops. The State Emergency Service. They'll have to come from Whale Head—and the chopper from Sydney.'

But as he spoke a gust of wind slammed across the face of the cliff and the truck seemed to shudder. And Jenny saw something in the side window facing upward. A face.

A dog? Definitely. Fawn-coloured, with oversized white ears. Staring straight up at them?

Surely no one would drive a truck over the cliff with a dog inside.

Unless it was a suicide attempt?

'How old's Charlie?' she demanded. 'He must be inside the truck as well. Or thrown out and in the sea?'

'He's eighty if he's a day. Dammit, Jenny, Charlie *must* be behind the wheel.'

'I'll go down.'

'Are you kidding? We need to wait for help.'

'By which time the truck might have fallen. You have ropes in the back of the ambulance. I can abseil down.'

'You? Abseil?'

'It's what I do for a hobby,' she said, and she managed a smile. 'You didn't read my résumé, huh? That bag I tucked into the back of the truck yesterday—it has my abseiling gear.'

'You're kidding.' He shook his head, staring down at the truck again. Its movement had them both almost mesmerised. 'Jen, we've been desperate,' he said as he stared. 'Pete'll be out of action for months, and that's left me with just Chris and Doc. Pierson to help in an emergency. The first page of your application confirmed you had a pulse and qualifications. You were therefore hired.'

She managed a chuckle at that. 'Wow, I'm flattered.'

It was Saturday evening. Jenny had arrived in Willhua on Thursday, planning to start work on Monday, but Gary had spent time with her the day before. So far she'd liked what she'd seen. Gary was in his sixties, he had the beginnings of arthritis in his hands which held him back, but he seemed skilled, sensible and friendly.

He was a far cry from the last man she'd worked for. Bottom-feeding toerag.

Now, however, was not the time to dwell on the humiliation she'd walked away from in Sydney. Now was the time to focus on the guy in the truck. It was late and the light was fading. If she was going down she had to go now.

'I can't abseil,' Gary said. 'Not when it's this steep, and as your boss, I'm not sure I should allow it. Pete always does the climbing stuff. I'll ring Doc Pierson. He'll know what to do.'

'Call him by all means,' Jen said. 'But I'm going. If Charlie's had a heart attack, if he's bleeding out...' Already she was seeing this Charlie-the-farmer as a real person, not just a random accident victim. 'There's no choice.'

'Can you do it without risk?'

That was a fair question. Safety was drilled into paramedics from their earliest training— *Do not put yourself in danger.* The last thing you wanted was to add yourself to the roll call of dead or injured. But still, almost every paramedic eventually faced situations where risk had to be weighed.

She was weighing risk now. It looked a simple abseil. The driver's side of the truck was facing upward and the door looked clear. She couldn't see the driver, but the dog was looking out of the window. She was assuming the driver had slumped sideways.

Deirdre had said the car had been weaving all over the road. So...drunk? Stroke? Heart attack? Diabetic hypo?

And at any minute the truck might fall.

Yes, there was a risk, but it was a risk worth taking.

'I'll push back if the truck moves,' she told Gary. 'But I might be able to clear an airway, or stop bleeding, at least do the basics. If you could lower the stretcher, maybe I could attach it to the tree, get it steady, even get him out.'

'By yourself? In your dreams. But could we stabilise the truck?' Bob sounded doubtful. 'With the bushfires down in Victoria and the amount of rain we've had here, our local fire crew figured they were needed more down south. They left as part of the interstate response. We need a crane, but Jodie Adams has the only crane in Willhua, and her family has dinner with her mum in Whale Head on Saturday nights. She won't be back yet. Could we use the ropes to attach the truck to…?' But then he paused and stared around him. There were no trees near the road. It was a narrow strip of bitumen and the cliff rose steeply behind them. 'To the ambulance?'

'We could try,' she said. 'But that's a heavy truck. I doubt the ropes'd hold—or they'd pull our truck over.'

What had she got herself into? she thought. She'd just come from a huge paramedic service in Southern Sydney, and her team had been multiskilled. Here there was no one but herself and Gary.

Willhua was a tiny coastal town that attracted retirees, plus people who liked out-of-the-way places—scuba divers, surfers, a paragliding community who used the wind to fly along the lonely but spectacular cliff faces. It had a tiny hospital that existed only because the place was so remote.

Pete, the paramedic she was replacing, had smashed his foot while surfing off the rocks a few weeks ago. With him out of action, the little town had been desperate for a replacement. The temporary job had seemed an ideal solution, a place to come and nurse her broken heart—or at least her shattered pride—but right now what she wanted was her huge metropolitan rescue team.

'We could use a tractor,' she said now. 'Or something else heavy to hold things firm. But with this wind there's no time to wait till they arrive. Once it's dark I can't abseil. But ring everyone you can think of. Meanwhile I'm going down.'

'Jen, I'm your superior. What'll people say if I let you go?'

'They'll say I have every certificate available in advanced abseiling skills,' Jen said, with only an inward qualm at the slight…deception. As far as she knew, there were no certificates available for advanced or any other level of abseiling. 'It's only sensible.'

'The risks…'

'I won't go into the truck,' Jen promised. 'And

we have gear in the ambulance.' She did have her abseiling kit—one of the things that had attracted her to this place had been the opportunity to practice her climbing skills, and she'd guessed, given the popularity of this place for windsurfers and paragliders, that she might even get to use her skills for professional reasons.

But to help someone in a truck in this position...

At least she could get to him, she reasoned. 'I will take care,' she told Gary. 'We can't just stand here and do nothing. Agreed?'

Gary stared at her for a long moment. 'I should go myself,' he said at last. 'But...' He shook his head. 'I can't.'

'What, thirty years in the service and you've never learned how to clamber down cliffs like a rock crab?' Jenny said, and tried a smile. 'But isn't that the reason I was employed, to add to the skill set your service offers? Are you happy to help me?'

He stared at her again, thinking. 'I'd like you to wait for Doc. And for Chris. Either of them might know what to do. We need more people than me to control things.'

They both stared down at the truck again and another gust shook the tree holding the vehicle.

'Yeah, but Charlie can't wait,' Jenny said. 'Let's go.'

* * *

It was eight o'clock on a Saturday night and Dr Rob Pierson had just disconnected from his nightly call to the hospital at Brisbane Central. The response had been pretty much the same response he'd had every night for the last four years.

'No change at all, Dr Pierson. Your wife's as comfortable as we can make her.'

Dammit, why wouldn't they let her go?

He stared into the empty fireplace—it was cool enough to light a fire but he couldn't be bothered. He'd have a drink and head to bed in a minute. Or maybe he'd check on Jacob again, then head through and do a fast check on his patients.

Willhua's official doctor's residence had been built to make a doctor's life easy. There was therefore a door in the hall that led through to the rear of the hospital's nurses' station. Rob had also rigged up a video and monitor. If four-year-old Jacob called out, or if he moved from bed, Rob or one of the nurses on call could be through here in seconds.

It wasn't a perfect system—Rob's parents-in-law had raised it in court as yet another reason why Rob shouldn't have custody—but the judge had come down on Rob's side. Willhua was desperate to keep its doctor. Not only the nurses, but almost every local was only too ready to drop everything and take on Jacob's care in an emergency, so somehow the system worked.

Willhua wasn't all that prone to emergencies anyway, apart from the occasional paraglider or windsurfer who did something stupid. Such casualties were mostly airlifted to Sydney. The hospital was thus pretty much a glorified nursing home for the retirees who made up half the population. But Rob had a local farmer in to-night who was recovering from snakebite, plus he'd admitted a young mum with mastitis. She wasn't desperately sick, but she was exhausted, and admitting her might force her lazy husband to step up and take care of the other two kids for a couple of days.

It wasn't cutting-edge medicine but he liked it, though the ongoing conflict with his in-laws was doing his head in.

Maybe he should give in, he thought grimly. Head back to Brisbane. Sit by Emma's bed for the how many years she might live like this?

He couldn't do it, to himself or to Jacob. But his thoughts were bleak, and when the phone rang it was almost a relief.

'Doc?' He knew Gary's voice well, and the single word conveyed trouble.

'What's up?'

'We have a truck near the bottom of Devil's Pass. We think it's Charlie Emerson. Deirdre McConachie called it in, said the truck was weaving like he was drunk. It went straight over. It's caught halfway down but not stable. Chris is caught up on the far side of the valley, you know the fire crew's still down in Victoria and Jodie's tow truck's unavailable. Meanwhile we think Charlie's stuck halfway down the cliff.'

His heart sank.

Safety had been drilled into him since medical school, and safety would be on the line here. There was a time when he'd have taken risks almost without thinking, but being sole parent to a four-year-old changed things. With Emma's parents seemingly watching every move, almost paranoid in their need to protect their grandson, his appetite for risk was pretty much nil.

Pete, the paramedic who'd injured his foot, had been adept at cliff rescues, but Gary had reluctantly agreed some years back that he couldn't do it. And this new woman they'd just employed? Gary had done the interview. Could she help or would he be forced to intercede? On his own?

'Ring South Sydney Air Rescue,' he said bluntly. 'Get a chopper.'

'I already have, but they're caught up on another job and there's no time to wait.' There was suddenly an odd note of pride in Gary's voice. 'But our Jenny...the new lass...damned if she's not an abseiler. She's rigging herself a harness and she's about to head down.'

'She can't!'

'She says she can, and I believe her. Truck's about to fall, Doc. She says she won't take stupid risks and Charlie must be bad. Can you get someone to ring round for tractors? A few guys with decent ropes. Just in case. Then come?'

So there was no choice. 'I need to hand over Jacob's care but I'll use the car phone to do the rest,' he told him. 'Stop her until I get there and that's an order.'

'The lady's got a mind of her own,' Gary said, and the pride was there again. 'And you know what? The way she looked at the whole set-up… the way she's acting… I'm thinking she knows what she's doing a lot more than the pair of us put together.'

The abseil down the cliff had been relatively straightforward. The tricky part now was to reach the person inside the truck without adding to its instability.

There was also a dog, and the dog wasn't helping one bit.

The driver's door was almost horizontal, a flat plane, and as soon as she reached the truck Jenny could see down inside the cab.

Charlie—or at least she assumed it was Charlie—was slumped across the seats. His legs were still almost in the driver's seat position but he'd slide sideways so his head was on the passenger side. There was blood on his chest and on his face. The left side of his shirt was ripped and she could see a jagged wound on his upper arm.

The dog was clambering over his body, seeing Jen, desperate to get to this newcomer. A corgi? This was a complication she didn't need. The dog, too, looked bloody, but she had no idea whether it was Charlie's blood or its own.

As a trained paramedic Jen had been in situations before where a dog had been protective of an injured owner. Her heart sank, but she couldn't get to Charlie without dealing with the dog.

She had ropes. There were light lines in the gear kit attached to her back.

First priority dog?

'What's happening?' Gary yelled from up on the road.

'I'm getting the dog out,' she called back. Gary would understand the situation.

'Hey,' she said, turning back to the cab's occupant, not sure if he could hear her but talking anyway. 'Hold still there, Charlie, rescue's happening.'

She hoped.

First things first. She steadied herself as much

as she could, finding leverage for her legs, almost stability. And then she attacked the door.

Opening a truck door when it was the right way up was relatively easy, unless it was damaged. This door wasn't damaged but, the way it was lying, it needed to be hauled up to open, a dead weight. Jen was fit, but even so it was a challenge, more so because the minute she got it open the dog was in her face.

'Stay,' she said firmly as she struggled. 'Good boy. Stay still!'

And, amazingly, he did. He was on Charlie's body, and he was leaning out to greet her, his tongue lolling. It was an impossible situation but at least he wasn't vicious.

She hauled the door up further until finally its own weight caused it to slam back against the truck tray. Okay, she now had a clear entrance, but her access was still blocked by the dog.

She grabbed one of the cords she had in her kit and reached in, then gave herself a moment to steady, reassure the dog.

'Now, mate, come on out,' she told him and tugged.

And he did. The position of the truck must have given him a false sense of security, its side forming a flat surface. He scrambled out, and Jen saw grazing along his side—a lot of grazing. Blood. Lacerations. He whimpered as she hauled, but she had no choice.

'Sorry, mate,' she told him. 'But we need to get your master safe first.'

She moved herself further along the tray and dragged the dog with her. The side of the truck formed part of a rusty crate. As she pulled, the dog lurched off the door onto the crate's wire sides. There was a yelp of pain, but she had no time for further reassurance. Once the dog was stable she tied him fast and left him. If the truck fell, the dog would go too, but there was no choice.

And now Charlie. With the corgi out of the way she could get into the truck, but she had to be so careful. Her weight could easily make the difference, causing the truck to slide.

She steadied herself, fighting to find a decent toe-hold, allowing the ropes to hold all her weight when all her instincts were screaming at her to use the truck to balance herself.

Finally she leaned in.

Charlie looked grey. In his eighties, small, almost wizened, his face looked ghastly. 'Pain,' he gasped. 'I can't…bear…'

Pain from where? In this situation it was impossible to tell.

But stopping the bleeding had to be her first priority. How much blood had he lost? Was it his blood or the dog's? In the fading light it was impossible even to guess.

'Are you Charlie?' she asked as she gloved.

'I…yeah.'

'I'm Jen, Willhua's new ambulance officer, here to get you out of here,' she told him. 'But let's get you a bit tidier first.' She was forming a pad and applying pressure as she spoke, assessing, thinking fast.

She had to get him out, but to pull him out when he was already grey with pain…

'Hey, you'll be okay.' They were easy words, but how to make them true?

By the look on his face, the pain he was feeling was excruciating. In the back of her mind was the description of him weaving on the road and then driving straight over. Heart problem? It had to be a possibility, but aspirin was out of the question here. She had no way of assessing internal bleeding. Risks, though, had to be weighed and tugging him out of the truck without pain relief might well kill him.

But giving pain relief in this situation was risky, too. Even finding a vein would be hard. Respiratory depression was problematic and pain might be coming from anywhere, but somehow he had to be dragged out.

Okay. Decision made. Low dose morphine.

'I'm giving you something for the pain,' she

told him. 'We'll wait for a couple of moments to let it take effect and then get you out of here.' When she'd figured out how.

The injection went home. Charlie was still staring at her with eyes dilated with terror and she grabbed his hand and held, hard.

And then, despite the slight tremors of the truck, despite the knowledge that the tree could give way at any minute, Jen forced herself into the space her training had instilled. She took a long look at the truck, at the guy's position. The passenger side seemed damaged. The door must have been bashed open as it slid or tumbled down the cliff. Where the door should have been, she could only see broken glass, torn metal and rockface.

She didn't want Charlie to talk any more than he must, but this was vital.

'Charlie, was anyone else in the truck with you?'

And his terror seemed to grow. His eyes swivelled to see, and he made himself whisper.

'My...dog?' His voice faltered and he looked pleadingly up at her, as if trying to say something more but there was no strength. 'My mate, Bruce?'

'Is Bruce your dog?'

'He was just...just here.'

And Jenny relaxed just a touch. 'He's safe,'

she told him. 'I got him out. Now, let's get you out too.'

But how? His legs weren't trapped—thank heaven for small mercies. He must have been cut in the fall, she thought. Maybe there were crush injuries, but underlying everything...what? There was no smell of alcohol. Had a medical event caused this? Was there an underlying heart attack?

She pulled back so she was leaning out of the cab and grabbed her radio. 'Gary?'

'Reading.'

'He seems alone apart from his dog. You'll have seen me tie the dog to the tray? Nothing's holding Charlie in the cab but we need to get him out fast. Bleeding, lacerations, severe pain, possibly internal injuries, possibly prior, maybe a heart attack?'

There was a sharp intake of breath as Gary processed the implications, but he was professional enough to move straight to the practical. 'Doc's here, on his way down now. He's bringing the stretcher'

Yeah? That was like a shot of adrenalin all on its own. Gary had organised the ambulance floodlight, so the deepening dusk was now alleviated by the artificial light. She swivelled to look up the cliff and yes, a figure was near the edge, leaning back, his feet finding a foothold on the cliff face. The ropes around him, the way he held himself, told her that here was someone else who was capable of abseiling. And by his side Gary was lowering a stretcher rig, lined up for a vertical rescue.

She'd spent yesterday browsing the ambulance set-up, familiarising herself with what this service could offer. Because Willhua was remote and a lot of its retrievals were from the beach, they carried a stretcher rig. It consisted of a light metal frame with webbing, with maximum hand holds, fastenings to secure a patient if they needed to cross rough ground, with the rigging needed if the patient had to be hauled upward.

Such a rescue should wait for the specialised chopper team from Sydney, but Charlie's breathing said they didn't have the luxury of waiting. She swung herself back to the cab.

'Charlie,' she said and lifted his hand again and held. Shifting him before they had the stretcher in position seemed fraught—any movement could send the truck down. All she could do right now was reassure, reassure, reassure. 'Doc's on his way. Doc Pierson—you know him? They say he's good. He's bringing a stretcher so we can get you out.'

'But…' The man's eyes were wild with fear, searching the cabin.

'We have your dog safe,' she repeated. 'Everything's okay except you seem to have broken some ribs. We'll get you to the hospital.'

He closed his eyes and for a sickening moment she thought he'd gone into cardiac arrest. But her fingers found his wrist and his pulse was still there, weak and thready but constant.

'Here.' The voice came from above her and she almost jumped. She swivelled and here he was, the doctor she'd met for a brief moment when she'd arrived for her interview.

She'd come to Willhua a week ago in answer to the job advertisement, and Gary had organised an interview. This doctor had been there. They'd therefore met—just—but two minutes after her introduction there'd been a call. Someone had arrived at the hospital having sliced their hand while cooking.

'It's bleeding like stink and I can't stop it,' she'd heard the woman say via the speaker phone. The doctor—Rob Pierson—had apologised and left in a hurry.

'You gotta get used to that here,' Gary had told her. 'It's a small town, so any drama we all stop everything. Luckily dramas don't happen all that often.'

Like on the first day of her first shift? The local policeman was caught up with an assault, and now, what had the doctor had to abandon to get here?

Regardless, she was blessedly glad to see him. What was more, he was moving as if he was accustomed to this type of situation. He'd swung down the cliff fast, with the stretcher attached by harness and the blue lines she recognised. He was now almost at eye level. With black hair, tanned, sun-weathered skin and a long, lithe body, he looked superbly fit, the type of guy she'd met during her climbing training. Now he was meeting her gaze, with eyebrows raised. Questions were in his dark eyes though, not in his voice.

But she knew what he was asking. Condition? Urgency? There was no room in the cab for him to take her place to examine, and no time either. Demanding a condition report within the patient's hearing was also problematic. But that one questioning glance contained trust. One professional to another.

Her gaze met his and held, and she saw that he got it. The urgency.

This guy wasn't so old, mid-thirties maybe, and in her work Jen had often found that younger doctors were suspicious of paramedics' ability. Rob Pierson, though, glanced in at Charlie— a cursory glance, given the lack of light in the cab—then looked at Jen. Jen nodded and the decision seemed to be made.

'Harness coming in,' he said briefly. 'Attach the line. Two minutes.'

Right. Deep breath.

Pulling a grown man out of a truck in this position seemed impossible. She didn't think she could do it. But they had to get him out of here, and the harness was a godsend. It was hard to get it fitted, but somehow she did, and with that came a slight lessening of tension. Now he was harnessed, the blessed safety lines fixed, all she had to do was shift him upward so if the truck plunged he wouldn't follow.

All she had to do? Shifting a dead weight was easier said than done.

'Swap.' Rob's order was a curse snap and she obeyed instinctively. If she knew how to achieve this she would have fought him, but she was only hoping he might have more of an idea than she did.

She backed out, using her climbing ropes to steady her, conscious all the time of not putting weight on the truck.

She risked another glance at Rob as she emerged from the cab. The unspoken message, one medic to another. Situation dire.

'On my signal, tell Gary full strength on my ropes,' he told her. 'You control Charlie's line, using it to help pull as much as you can.' And then, as he moved closer, he spoke to Charlie.

'Charlie, mate, this is Rob Pierson. Dr Pierson—you know me. We need to get you out of here, but we need your help. I'm going to link my hands under your shoulders and pull, but do you reckon you can push a bit with your legs? I know it'll hurt like hell, but a nice comfy stretcher's waiting.'

Could he do it? It was almost a vertical lift. Jen shifted a little on her ropes, ready to grab what she could if—when—he emerged. The safety lines attached to Charlie would help, but not much. She couldn't see how...

But he did. One moment Rob was bent over—all she could see was his back. The next he was pulling back and, miraculously, Charlie was in his hold.

What sort of Herculean strength...?

But there was no time for questions. As Charlie emerged she grabbed his thighs and helped manoeuvre him. Rob had set the stretcher up so it was hanging just above the tray. In less time than she would have believed possible they had him fastened, and Rob was calling upward.

'Bring us up!'

There must be more people on the clifftop by now, Jen realised, because the ropes tightened instantly. Rob moved into position beside the stretcher, attaching himself, stabilising it as it moved. Then, with the utmost care from those above—that'd be Gary, she thought, even if he couldn't abseil he'd know the drill—Rob and the stretcher were on their way upward.

The whole process had been so fast she felt dazed. She let herself hang for a moment, using her feet to steady herself, but taking a moment to let her breath subside to normal.

And then the dog whined.

She'd almost forgotten him. Bruce, the dog. He was crouched low, flattened on the wire crate. Another gust of wind hit and the truck shuddered again. She couldn't leave him.

'Another harness,' she yelled upward.

'Someone else?' She heard alarm in Gary's voice.

'Dog,' she called. All attention up on the road had to be on Charlie, but she'd promised. 'He's too big for me to carry but I reckon a harness might work.'

And Gary must have agreed because a rope came down, with a harness.

It was a stupid fit—a human harness—but the dog seemed almost paralysed with pain and fear. She hooked the harness around his rear and the corgi looked up at her with limpid trusting eyes that made her melt.

'It's okay, boy,' she said softly. 'Let's get you to your master.'

And somehow she managed it. She had whoever was up the cliff pull gently, she swung on her rope with the dog in her arms, the harness took her weight from her rear, and she steadied Bruce and herself by finding footholds as she rose.

And, moments later, she and the dog were on the road.

This was a very different scenario than the one she'd left, what, half an hour back? There were people everywhere. Gary and Rob were crouched over the stretcher. A guy in a policeman's uniform—was this Chris?—was in charge of the rope pulls, and there were at least half a dozen locals looking desperate to help.

Thank heaven. She let herself slump on the road for a moment, cradling the dog, letting herself believe that the drama was over. Then she rose and carried the dog across to the stretcher.

If anything Charlie looked even worse than when she'd last seen him. Rob was setting up a syringe. Gary was trying to fit an oxygen mask, but the old guy was fighting him.

'Bruce,' he gasped.

'Hey, we have him.' She knelt by the stretcher, holding the corgi so he could see him. 'Here he is. Bruce.'

The old man's eyes widened in hope. He stared wildly—and then he looked straight past her.

'Stumpy,' he stammered, and he tried to

raise his hand to pat his dog. 'I knew she… But where's…where's Bruce?'

'Who's Bruce?' Rob snapped, his voice urgent.

'Best…best mate,' Charlie whispered—and stopped breathing.

CHAPTER TWO

AFTER THAT THINGS got a bit blurry. Someone took the dog from her, and the three of them went into overdrive. Full CPR, defibrillation, the works. There was total silence from the onlookers as they worked; maybe every one of them was doing what Jen was doing. Pleading. Please…

And, blessedly, on the third shock there was a pulse. Thready, weak but glorious. He was still unconscious, but with a pulse anything was possible.

'We need to get to the hospital, fast,' Rob snapped to Gary. 'I need equipment, lights, sirens—Gary, can you give us an escort? I need—'

But… 'Bruce,' Jen said out loud. She was leaning back on her heels. This had been so close. She'd been feeling relieved but now…

'Bruce?' They were suddenly all looking at her.

'Down in the truck,' she said, trying to figure things out as she spoke. 'Charlie was calling for Bruce and I assumed he was worrying about his dog. He said, "My mate, Bruce. My dog." I'd already pulled the dog out. I asked if Bruce was his dog and he seemed to agree but…' She closed her eyes for a millisecond, then she rose and crossed to a guy who was holding the dog she'd hauled up the cliff.

The corgi was lying passively at the guy's feet, its sides bloodstained, eyes wide with fear.

'Hey,' she said softly as she approached. She knelt and raised her hand to let the dog smell her, then gently fondled the spot most dogs loved, right behind the ear. And as she did she manoeuvred the dog's collar so she could read the faded rusty disc.

It said 'Stumpy'.

And Jen's hands did a fast check in the fading light and found confirmation.

Stumpy was a she.

'What gives?' The doctor—Rob—was suddenly by her side. He must have seen the colour drain from her face. 'Jen?'

'I assumed Bruce was this dog,' she whispered. 'But this one's a bitch and her name's Stumpy. And…and Charlie didn't actually say Bruce was a dog. He said…my mate.'

And he got it. 'So that leaves Bruce, dog or man, unaccounted for?' Rob's hands gripped her shoulders. 'You saw the inside of the truck,' he said in a voice that steadied her all by itself. It was firm, emotionless, demanding that she become professional again. 'Is there any way someone could have been thrown out?'

'I… Maybe?' she managed. 'The passenger door looked to be ripped off.' She closed her eyes, hauling the visual of the inside of the truck back into her mind. 'There was a seatbelt though. Undone.'

'If he wasn't wearing it…'

'I guess.'

And they both stared out over the cliff, into the deepening dusk.

'Okay, moving on. Let's leave the self-blame for later, Jen—and there's no need anyway. Even if we knew someone else was down there, we couldn't have done any more than we've done. Chris!' Rob called to the policeman. 'There's a possibility of someone else down there. Dog or man, we're not sure, but we need to assume it's a man. Name of Bruce. It's too dark for anyone else to climb down, and no use at all if they're in the sea. Can you get onto neighbours, anyone who might know who this Bruce is? Meanwhile, we need to get Charlie to the hospital. Come on, Jennifer, let's go.'

'Doc, I'll put the dog in the truck.' It was the guy who'd been holding Stumpy. 'Front seat? I assume you guys will be travelling in the back.

Charlie'll want his dog when he wakes up, and that cut on its side…it'll probably need stitches. Doc?'

'Because I'm doctor for everyone?' Rob said bleakly. 'Macca, we can't take the dog.'

'Limp as a biscuit, not causing any trouble,' the guy—Macca—told them. 'And she…she's gotta go somewhere. I don't know what to do with a bleeding dog.'

'Fine,' Rob said wearily. 'Gary, if it's okay by you…'

'I'll need to clean the truck out anyway, and the only alternative's your nice, clean car,' Gary said. 'Someone else'll bring that in, but who knows when? We can hardly leave the dog here.'

Rob sighed, but there was no time to argue.

Gary drove. He knew the curves of this cliff road like the back of his hand, and the ambulance moved as fast as he could while still allowing Jen and Rob to work in the rear. Rob worked on Charlie, monitoring his every breath. Jen knew she'd be needed if that breathing stopped, but it faltered on, and she had time to catch her own breath.

This was her first job, and she felt that she'd failed spectacularly. Rule number two, after personal safety, was to ascertain number of casualties.

The radio crackled into life and Gary called

back, 'This'll be the chopper update. There was no availability when I called. Can you take it, Jen? Concentrating here.'

He must be, Jen thought. The curves here were almost hairpin.

She flicked her radio into life and switched it to the main channel.

'South Coast Emergency Response Centre to Willhua First Response, do you copy?'

South Sydney Air Rescue. Her crew.

That was where she should be now, but this wasn't the time for regrets. She was needed just where she was.

'Willhua Paramedics, copy, loud and clear,' she said now into her radio. 'Status?'

'Hey, it's our Jen.' She recognised the operator and Donna obviously recognised her. 'You down a cliff already?'

'Transferring critical care to Willhua hospital,' she said.

And Donna got it—the tension, the unspoken need for urgent action. 'Crew's still half an hour away,' she said. 'We have co-ordinates of the crash scene. You want them to change route and pick up from the hospital?'

'Tell them he'll need transfer,' Rob told her. He was adjusting Charlie's oxygen mask and his face was grim. They both knew that if Charlie was to survive he'd need the specialist treatment of a major city hospital. 'But priority needs to be this Bruce.'

Jen nodded. He didn't have to go further.

'Donna, there's a strong possibility there's someone else on the cliff, on the rocks below or in the sea,' she told her. 'Our guy—Charlie—was calling for someone called Bruce before he lost consciousness. The police are making enquiries, but for now we need to assume Bruce is someone missing. The truck's on its side. Possibility someone's trapped underneath? We don't know, and it's too dark to climb down again.'

'Roger that,' Donna said, efficient and businesslike. 'I'll get the chopper there as soon as possible. You take care of your guy and stop worrying about the rest.'

'We'll also need transfer for Charlie,' she said.

'He'll need stabilisation first,' Rob said, loud enough for Donna to hear. 'There's probably time for the crew to search the cliff.'

'Roger that,' Donna said again. 'Good luck.'

What followed was an hour of futile fighting. A fight where everything Jen had ever learned in her medical past was called into play.

An hour where she learned that Rob Pierson was almost as skilled as the best emergency physicians she'd ever worked with.

When she was fourteen, the grandma Jen had

loved and lived with had had a major stroke. Her parents, adventurers, wanderers, pretty much selfish to the core—they still were—had reluctantly flown home, but after a month they'd decided that Jen could cope.

And Jen had. During the next few years she'd juggled schoolwork with living with and caring for the frail old lady, and during that time she'd seen the best side of nursing. The medical care given to her grandmother by the district nurses had been amazing, and the teenaged Jen had never had a doubt that this was where her career lay. Her grandma had died just as she'd started her nursing training.

But during her parents' sporadic visits she'd also been introduced to other skills. Abseiling, speed climbing, bouldering—she was enough her parents' child to learn and love them all. So as she'd finished training and started working as a nurse in a Sydney hospital emergency department, another desire had come to the fore. She'd watched the paramedics come in and out of the emergency rooms, she'd seen the care they gave, and she'd thought…why not?

She'd been accepted into paramedic training and she'd never regretted it.

But her nursing training was still there, and now, as they arrived at Willhua's hospital, as she realised there was only one nurse on duty and

Cathy was already overloaded, and as Charlie's heart faltered yet again, it made sense to tell them her qualifications and offer to help.

So for the next hour she assisted Rob as best she could. She watched and worked as Rob put everything he could into saving this old man's life.

But it was no use. When finally Charlie's injuries, or Charlie's heart, or the combination of everything the old man had gone through, finally overwhelmed his frail body, when Rob finally stood back from the table, his face blank with defeat, she felt like weeping. And she felt like hugging him—this doctor who'd worked so hard.

Of course she didn't. She didn't even know him, but she'd seen how hard he'd fought and she wanted...what?

The emotions of the past weeks plus the tension of the day were suddenly threatening to overwhelm her. She didn't know what she wanted.

For there to be a world where the sky didn't fall? Where toerag bosses didn't betray in the worst possible way? Where Charlie wasn't dead? Where the unknown Bruce was safe and well.

'I'm so sorry,' she said, and he closed his eyes and his shoulders sagged.

'Useless, useless, useless,' he muttered and the urge to hug him was even greater.

What was it with this man? She'd watched him swing down the abseiling line and thought he looked like some sort of hero in a movie—tall, lithe, dark-haired and dark-eyed, abseiling with ease, a man in charge of his world. But now he looked shocked and numb—like this was personal? Had Charlie been a friend?

And then she remembered something Gary had said, at that interview when he'd been called away.

'Doc works too hard. We're lucky to have him, he's a damn fine doctor. Bloody tragedy about his wife, though. He and the kiddie… Well, life kicks you around, that's for sure.'

Had his wife died in an accident as well?

'What a waste,' he said now, heavily, and then opened his eyes and looked at her. 'But his rescue was down to you, Jen. You got there when he was conscious, you got pain relief into him and he knew he was being cared for. Heaven knows if that truck's still in place—it could well have plummeted by now. And now, assisting with this… You've done great, Jen. Willhua's lucky to have you.'

Willhua was lucky to have *him*, she thought, but she didn't say it. The memory of Darren showering her with compliments was still fresh and raw, and something inside her cringed.

'It's my job,' she said a little too curtly. 'I just wish…'

She stopped and looked down at Charlie's face. In death he looked peaceful and there was something about him… An old man. Had it been his time?

And as if he knew what she was thinking, Rob reached out and placed a hand on her shoulder. He did it lightly, almost a casual contact, but something made her feel that right now he needed the touch as much as she did.

'Charlie's been a loner almost all his life,' he told her. 'I have no idea if he has any relatives around here. Or friends. I've seen him twice in the five years I've practiced here. The last time he came in was a year ago, for an infected leg. He'd ripped it on barbed wire and hadn't bothered to clean it. While he was here I insisted on basics, including a blood pressure check. It was through the roof, but he wouldn't have a bar of treatment. I sent him home with prescriptions, instructions and an appointment for follow-up but I suspect he ignored the lot.'

And then his grip on her shoulder tightened— a reassurance, a certainty? 'All I'm saying, Jen, is that we fought damned hard, but some choices were his.'

'But this Bruce? I should have…'

The pressure remained. 'You made decisions based on the information you had, and you did really well. The chopper's doing the rest now.'

By silent consensus they moved out of the room. Charlie's body needed to be dealt with, but there was no rush. They could give themselves—and Charlie—space while they talked of the future. As they closed the door behind them, Rob glanced at his watch.

'Surely there'll be news by now,' he said softly. 'This Bruce... But meanwhile, what happened to the dog you rescued?'

She managed a rueful smile, trying to shake off the desolation of what had just happened. 'Stumpy? Our next patient? Gary put her on the passenger seat of the ambulance. He couldn't take her home—he tells me his wife's allergic—but he's popped her into the hospital laundry. She'll need treatment. In the morning, I guess? Does Willhua run to a vet?'

He sighed. 'It does not,' he said heavily. 'If there's any emergency vet work, the locals call on me. I'll take a look at her now, but she can't stay here.'

'What, not prepared to admit her under your bed card?' They'd moved on, but the presence of death was still around them. 'I'll... I'll take care of her until someone claims her,' she said. 'I could use...some company.'

'What, you're lonely? Do you know anyone here?'

'Not a sausage.' She tried summoning a smile she was far from feeling. 'My landlady seems crabby but my studio at the back of her place has a garden which she says I'm free to use. Stumpy might help me settle in.'

He was looking at her curiously. 'Just like that?'

'Just like that,' she agreed. 'So…moving on?'

He nodded, taking her lead. 'Okay. We need to find out what's happened to this Bruce, and we need to check out Stumpy.'

'Gary told me you have a little boy,' she said, looking at his strained, tired face. 'Is he okay alone?'

'He's not alone. We have a great system,' he told her. 'We have video and alarms set up for sound and movement in his room—it's linked to monitors at the nurses' station, which is almost just through the wall, and if it's likely to be for any more than a few minutes I have Minnie.'

'Minnie?'

'Mrs Minnow. She a retired nurse and she lives next door,' he told her. 'And she's Jacob's and my own personal angel. My place is the original doctor's residence and when this place was built the doctor had five kids. So we've set up one of my spare rooms as Minnie's home away from home, right down to spare knitting. Minnie cares for Jacob during the day, but also during the night when I need her. She put on her moccasins and woolly robe, filled her hot-water bottle and pottered across the front lawn before I even left. Jacob's so used to it now I suspect he's delighted when he wakes to find her there.'

'It sounds ideal.'

'Some would think so,' he said, and strangely his voice suddenly sounded heavy. 'Others… well, there are some who'll never concede I can care for my own son.'

They split up then. He and Cathy needed to cope with the aftermath—the moving of Charlie's body to the morgue, the paperwork, the effort of finding relatives. Jen shouldn't even be here—she was officially off-duty. Actually she hadn't even officially started work yet, but who was noticing?

She needed to head back home, or where home was right now. It was a couple of blocks to Lorna's, but first…the dog.

She made her way to the hospital laundry, but paused as her phone rang. Frankie.

Frankie had been her best friend while she worked for the chopper service. She was still her best friend. Frankie had stood by her while her life had felt as if it was being ripped apart, had even pushed her to try and get her boss sacked instead of walking away. Even if he had been sacked though, the humiliation would still be with her, and in the end Frankie had accepted that decision.

Was Frankie with the retrieval crew? If so, she must have decided to make this call private, and part of her relaxed. If it was bad news Frankie would have made it official.

She stopped mid corridor and leaned against the wall. 'What gives?'

'You're not going to believe this,' Frankie told her. 'Bruce is a dog.'

'A dog.' Her body seemed to sag with relief. She'd been haunted by the vision of an injured man on the rocks below the cliff, someone who, if she'd asked the right questions earlier, could have been saved. Okay, she was being hard on herself—there'd been no time to do any more— but she'd still been haunted.

'A great big hairy dog,' Frankie was saying. 'I'm no expert but Mozzie's spent time on farms and he reckons he might be a bearded collie. He and Nico are trying to dry him off a bit.'

She knew Mozzie, but Nico? Was Nico her replacement in the crew?

'I'm not really surprised,' she said. 'We already rescued one dog that was with Charlie. Where was this one? Why didn't I see it?'

'He was curled up in a tight ball, hiding amongst rocks and scrub not far from that tree that the truck was initially caught on. He must have been thrown clear when it first went over the cliff. He's black and white—it was only because I caught a glimpse of the white hair that we found him. He would have been totally hidden from view when you pulled that guy out. Speaking of whom... Condition?'

'He's just died.'

It was a stark statement. Her voice seemed to echo in the corridor and there was a sharp intake of breath from her friend.

'Oh, no... I'm so sorry, love, and on your first day!'

'My first day's supposed to be Monday.'

'And you wanted a quiet life.' There was a pause and then Frankie went on. 'Our reports were that a fatality was likely,' she said, obviously deciding that professional brevity was the way to cope. Wasn't it always? 'Jen, we still have a problem. 'The Serious Crash Squad got mobilised when your local cop pinged this as a possible fatality. They're here now, but they don't want anything to do with the dog. They suggested we drop him off to you so the local vet can check him out.'

'Is he injured?'

'Not sure. Nico's having a look now, but I'd be surprised if he wasn't hurt. Pretty rough ground for a fall.'

'Who's Nico?' She had to ask.

'You're replacement on Red Watch.'

Ouch. That definitely hurt. She'd loved working with this team.

It couldn't matter—but there was something in Frankie's voice that piqued her interest…

'Is he nice?'

'He's Italian.'

Yeah, like that told her a lot. Sadly, however, they both needed to move on.

'Do you know if the local vet will be available?' Frankie was asking.

'There's no vet in Willhua.'

'Can he go to Charlie's family?'

'I have no idea who that might be. Frankie, can you take him on to Sydney? I seem to be stuck with the other one—Stumpy—and I can't cope with two injured dogs.'

And then she paused as Rob appeared in the corridor. 'Just a moment,' she told Frankie. 'Rob, Bruce turned out to be a dog. He's safe.'

'Well, that's a bit of good news.'

'Frankie, I need to go,' she told her friend. 'Stumpy's got lacerations and grazes, and Rob's going to help me sort her out.'

'Who's Rob?' And she heard a lightening of interest in her friend's voice. Which would be a lot more intense if she could see Rob, she thought. The guy was standing in the doorway, looking weary but also…hot? Definitely hot. A doctor who'd climbed down the cliff to rescue a dying man, who'd shown as much, or more, abseiling skill as she had, who'd fought with skill and desperation to save the life of an old man…

There must be a better descriptor than hot, she thought, but right now hot was all she could come up with.

'Cut it out,' she said, but it was as much to herself as it was to her friend. Dammit, Frankie was incorrigible—though she thought of how her own interest had pinged at the mention of the unknown Nico and she almost smiled. She and Frankie knew each other so well.

Now, however, was definitely not the time for an inquisition. Or thinking of the man standing in the doorway. 'But can you take Bruce?' she managed.

'I'll see what I can do.' There was a moment's hesitation then, 'There's already a discussion about having a dog in the chopper,' Frankie told her.

'But that would be a yes?' Jen said quickly. 'That's great. If and when we find relatives we can tell them he's in the best of hands and to contact you.'

'Jen…'

'I need to go,' she told her friend hurriedly. 'Love you.'

CHAPTER THREE

AFTER THAT THEY went straight back into work mode, only this time their patient was a dog.

Looking at the corgi from one side, it appeared there was no damage at all. 'She's just like the Queen's,' Cathy, the night nurse, said as she saw Rob carrying the injured dog through from the laundry to the theatre. The dog looked relatively young, with lovely fawn and white colouring and a gorgeous bushy tail. But her tail was hanging downward and her oversized ears seemed almost drooping. That, and the expression in her eyes, were a giveaway that something was badly wrong.

And as soon as the strong overhead lights went on they could see why.

She must have been hurled against the shattered side window, Jen thought. Her side was a gory mess. Most of the fur was torn away, her skin was grazed and bloody, and a long laceration ran almost from shoulder to the base of her ribs. It was still sluggishly bleeding.

In any other circumstances this dog should have been a priority, Jen thought, horrified. Instead she'd been tugged ruthlessly out of the truck, tied to the crate, hauled up the cliff—and then left alone in the hospital laundry. All of them had been too concerned with the drama around Charlie's survival to take more than a cursory interest.

But even injured, in pain, in a bewilderingly strange environment, she seemed passive, looking up at Jen and Rob with something that seemed almost like trust. She stood quietly on the bench as Rob examined her. Jen stood by her head, fondling her ears, speaking gently to her, and the dog seemed to almost melt into her hands. Her head sagged, and as Jen bent a little she lifted her snout and gave Jen's face a long, trusting lick.

And Jen's heart almost broke. 'Oh, she's lovely,' she breathed.

'Not from this angle, she's not,' Rob said grimly. 'This side's a mess. I can see embedded glass.'

'The nearest vet?'

'At Whale Head, and that's over an hour's drive along the cliffs. Even then, Ross is elderly and overworked. This'll be up to me. He will help by phone though. If I ring he'll give me anaesthetic doses and talk me through—he's done it before.'

'There's no one?' she asked, horrified.

'Do you know how hard it is to get any sort of medics to work outside the cities?'

'That's why you got me,' she said with an attempt at lightness, her hands still fondling the dog.

'And aren't we lucky that we did?' Cathy had followed them and was standing at the door, watching. 'Rob, Mike O'Connor's woken and his leg's bad. He was bitten by a snake yesterday,' she told Jen. 'He's recovering but his leg's very swollen.' She turned back to Rob. 'Could I have an order for pain relief?'

'I'll check him before we start here,' Rob said curtly. 'Hold the fort, Jen.'

And Jen was left…holding the fort…and wondering what sort of place she had landed herself in.

She thought briefly of her job with South Sydney Air Rescue. There her role had been clearly defined. Go with the ambulance or chopper to call outs. Treat at the scene and on the way to hospital. Maybe wait a while at the hospital—ramping, being stuck on the hospital ramp because of lack of hospital staff, had become common during the recent pandemic—but as soon as space was available the patient was wheeled through the doors and became Not Her Responsibility.

And her hours… She'd usually been rostered for eight-hour shifts, which occasionally had stretched a little longer, but nothing like this. To be called out when she wasn't even on duty, to do a traumatic retrieval, to be needed to assist in a hospital setting, and then to stay on to treat an injured dog… If she reported this to her union, officialdom would have a field day.

But as she stood and waited, speaking and crooning to the dog, rubbing her soft ears, she was suddenly hit by a wave of something that was almost excitement.

The last few weeks had been a muddle of confusion and humiliation. Almost every waking moment had seen her reliving the worst of Darren's betrayal, and her rush to get away had been driven by those emotions.

But tonight she'd been needed—she was still needed. Her skills had been tested. Her nursing training had mostly receded to the point where she'd thought it had almost been a waste, but tonight, even though Charlie had died, her skills had been front and centre again.

And this doctor…

He was skilled, empathic and…gorgeous?

Down, girl, she told herself, but a part of her was smiling ruefully at herself. After Darren she'd promised herself she'd never look at another male again—yeah, that was never going to happen, but now, after only weeks…

Right now it didn't exactly hurt, the feeling that as a paramedic she'd be working with Rob over and over again. Instead it seemed to have lifted something that had felt, for the last weeks, like it might take years to lift.

Because he was gorgeous? Her mind was back on that *hot* descriptor again.

'You can cut that out,' she told herself severely, but still…

She could hear him now. He'd obviously returned from his snakebite patient and was standing in the corridor talking on his phone. To someone called Ross.

The vet in Whale Head?

Yes.

She listened as Rob described Stumpy's condition, as he repeated instructions out loud, as he confirmed and reconfirmed.

This man was good, she thought, incisive, careful—caring?

He must be. To stay awake after midnight to treat a dog…

She thought of Cathy's request for pain meds for the snakebite patient. That'd be a normal thing for Rob, she realised, phone calls in the

middle of the night. Call outs. With no backup…
When was he ever off-duty?

Would the same apply to her? She was starting to realise that life in Willhua wouldn't be
eight-hour shifts either but, rather than being
dismayed, the thought filled her with a sense of
anticipation that had somehow pierced the con-
flicting emotions of the last few weeks.

And then Rob was back, standing beside her,
crouching a little so he was almost nose to nose
with the injured dog.

'Okay, girl, let's get you fixed,' he murmured.
'You trust us to get you feeling better?'

And the corgi's tongue slipped out again and
Rob also received a slurp, jaw to nose.

Rob grinned and Jen thought, *I agree. I'm with
Stumpy.*

The surgery took over an hour.

Jen was *not* an anaesthetist, but, 'It's you or
no one,' Rob told her. 'Ross has given us instructions and dosages and we can't leave glass
in her side.'

So she worked way past her skill level, monitoring depth of consciousness, breathing, heart
rate, while Rob worked on the dog's side.

It was lengthy, meticulous work. The shattered glass was clear, making it almost invisible,
and individual puncture marks had mostly been

obliterated by further damage—the dog must have crashed hard against her side. But if this had been a child Rob couldn't have been more painstaking. He searched and cleaned, searched and cleaned, and when the kidney dish held every shard he could possibly find he washed and washed and washed the entire area until he was almost satisfied.

'She'll need constant checking over the next few days,' he said grimly as finally he set about stitching the worst of the lacerations. 'If I've left any behind...'

'You've done your best,' she said, and he flashed a look at her.

'You know as well as I do that best is sometimes not good enough.' He sighed. 'Okay, let's get this dressed.' And then he hesitated. 'Jen, she can't stay here.'

'I know that.' She'd already accepted it. There was no way a dog could stay in a hospital setting—no way this man could be expected to do the obs an injured and sedated animal would require. 'She's coming home with me.'

'And home is?'

'At Lorna Dumet's. I'm renting a studio in her back garden.'

'Mrs Dumet.' He frowned. 'Um... Lorna... I'm not sure...'

'I'm not sure either,' Jen said and managed a

rueful smile. Her impression of Lorna was that of an officious, controlling matron, but the studio was self-contained and separate, with its own small garden.

'Will having a dog be okay with her?'

'There wasn't a no pets clause in my lease,' she said. 'But I'll run things past her tomorrow, just to keep things sweet.'

He cast her another doubtful glance. 'I guess it solves the problem for tonight at least,' he said slowly. 'You're happy to take her home now?'

'Of course.' And then she hesitated. Lorna's place was four or five blocks from the hospital, too far to walk with an injured dog, and her car was back at the ambulance station. The station was just as far as Lorna's. 'I guess... I can walk back and get the car and come and pick her up.' It was, though, two in the morning and the prospect wasn't exactly appealing.

'I'll take you,' Rob told her. 'If you're taking on Stumpy's care it's the least I can do. Give me a couple of minutes to check in on Jacob and Minnie, and I'll be right with you.'

They drove across the silent, sleeping town in near silence, with Jen cradling the drowsy Stumpy on her knee. This was hardly professional conduct, she thought, a medic carrying a patient in the front seat. No seat belt for Stumpy.

'Please don't crash,' she told Rob as the thought hit. 'We should have her in the back, properly secured. And do you have insurance for patient transport?'

'I wouldn't worry,' he said dryly. 'Anyone sues me—or you too, for that matter—then Willhua loses medics it can't do without. There are advantages to being irreplaceable.'

'Do you have no help at all?' she asked curiously and she saw his face relax a little.

'I do,' he told her. 'Willhua's last family doctor is still living here. Angus is over seventy, he's retired and wants nothing more than to spend his time growing vegetables, but in an emergency or when I need to have time off, he covers for me.'

'When you need to have time off?' she ventured, hearing a strange note in his voice. 'You mean holidays?'

'I wish. I need to spend time in Brisbane. My...' He hesitated and then seemed to change tack. 'Jacob needs to spend time with his grandparents—my wife's parents—and I...' But he didn't finish the sentence and she saw his hands tighten on the wheel.

There was obviously something behind that story, Jen thought, but there was no time now to unravel it, even if it was her business—which it wasn't.

They were pulling up outside Lorna's. The

house was a fastidiously manicured ode to pseudo-Georgian. Not a blade of grass ventured higher than its companions on the pristine lawn. Pansies and petunias lined up like well drilled soldiers along the driveway, and standard roses guarded the front fence. They were all in bud because as soon as the roses bloomed—and risked shedding a petal—they were clipped and delegated to the trash.

Not even the compost. The day she'd arrived, Jen had found Lorna dead-heading roses that clearly weren't dead. Intrigued, she'd offered to carry her cart to the compost heap—and snaffle a few on the way to put in her kitchenette.

'The bin, you mean,' Lorna had snapped. 'Why would I want compost? Filthy, smelly stuff.'

Now Lorna's front lights were blazing, and as they pulled up Jen could see two of the nearer rose bushes had buds that were daring to unfurl. She pretty much expected Lorna to dart out and be off with their heads. She grinned at the thought, and saw the query in Rob's eyes.

She explained and he chuckled as he lifted Stumpy out of the car.

'Yeah, I can imagine. You know, Lorna has… issues of her own. She can be a bit volatile. If you have any trouble, let me know.'

'I intend to keep out of the lady's way. I need

to use the side path to get to the studio, but I'm thinking I'll slink.'

That brought another chuckle. 'Okay. Let me help you slink, though. I'll carry Stumpy.'

She accepted with a certain amount of relief—the idea of carrying Stumpy while she fiddled with unfamiliar locks and door handles presented problems. So Rob followed with Stumpy as she led him down the side path.

They'd almost cleared the main house when the security lights blazed on. Thirty seconds later, as she fiddled with the lock of her front door, Lorna, resplendent in a flowery oriental bathrobe, banged out of her back door and surged across the lawn towards them.

'What do you think you're doing?' Her voice was a high-pitched screech. I said no men! It's in your lease. No men, young woman! I will not have it.'

Oh, for heaven's sake. Jen sighed. Her first impression of Lorna—that being her tenant was not going to be easy—suddenly multiplied by ten. But, before she could answer, Rob intervened.

'Good evening, Mrs Dumet,' he said pleasantly, and Lorna stopped in her tracks.

'Dr Pierson! What are you doing here?'

'Just helping Miss Roden home,' Rob told her, his tone still pleasant. 'She's caring for one of my patients overnight.'

He'd been standing back a little, waiting for Jen to open the door. She succeeded and flicked the light on, a porch light which, inconveniently, could only be activated from the inside. Light flooded the trio on the porch, and Lorna's jaw dropped.

'A dog,' she breathed.

'It's Charlie Emerson's dog,' Rob said mildly. 'Charlie died earlier this evening and Stumpy was injured. Miss Roden has kindly offered to care for her until we can locate Charlie's relatives.'

If he'd hoped to gain sympathy he was sadly mistaken. Jen, standing in the doorway, saw her landlady's face turn from indignation to downright anger.

'And you thought you could just bring it here. At two in the morning? Disturbing my sleep with your goings-on! I thought you'd be a quiet single woman who'd keep to herself, and that was the only reason I agreed to let my dear mother's studio. It's been empty since she died and I will not have goings-on...'

'By goings-on, do you mean living?' Rob asked, his voice still mild. He'd stepped forward a little, his body between Jenny and the woman who was stalking over the lawn. 'Lorna, we've talked about this before—reacting with anger. There's no need for anger tonight. Jenny's our much-needed ambulance officer and she's been doing her best to save a life tonight.'

'It's two in the morning! All the security lights came on. Outside my bedroom window!'

'If you want Jenny to stay, you may have to do something about that,' he told her. 'Jenny's an ambulance officer, so there will be out of hours calls. We all know how much the town needs another ambulance officer. It's been great that you've been able to give her somewhere to live.'

But his placatory tone didn't seem to be helping. Lorna was totally focused on Jenny and the dog. 'Well!' She put her hands on her hips and glared. 'Of all the effrontery... But to come here... With you... And a dog... There's no way she can have a dog here.'

'Mrs Dumet, I have my own yard on the other side of the studio,' Jen said, stepping forward. It was all very noble of Rob to stand between them, but this was her battle. 'I know I didn't ask about pets when I applied—I didn't intend to have one—but there's no pet ban in my lease and Stumpy's hurt. Her master's dead and she needs short-term care. If there are real problems, if you're allergic, if you really hate dogs, then I'll figure something tomorrow.'

'You figure something now.' She glowered at the two of them. 'And bringing a man here... Dr Pierson, you should be ashamed of yourself.'

This was escalating to the point of being ridiculous, Jenny thought. What was the lady suggesting—that she and Rob were heading indoors to have a spot of red-hot sex? She opened her mouth to speak, but Rob sent her a warning glance and spoke himself.

'We're sorry we've woken you, Lorna,' he said mildly. 'I'm dropping Jenny and the dog off now—I need to get back to Jacob—but could we talk about this in the morning?'

But Lorna Dumet was clearly nursing her grievance and had no intention of letting it go.

'I should never have let you have the studio in the first place,' she snapped. 'It's been empty since my dear mother died, and I don't want you sullying her memory. Charlie Emerson's dog... It'll be full of fleas, it'll bleed and heaven knows what else. Get it out of here or I'll call the police.'

'I hardly think Chris will be sympathetic,' Rob told her. 'He's dealing with Charlie's wrecked truck.'

'That's nothing to do with me. Get it out of here! And you too,' she screeched at Jen, indignation turning to rage. 'Pack your bags and go.'

'Jen...' Rob said in a low warning voice and Jen got it. This woman was out of control, at the point of hysteria, but both she and Rob had been trained in the art of de-escalation.

Sense said back off and let her calm down.

'I'll take you both home,' Rob said softly but urgently, watching Lorna's face turn from purple to puce. 'I'm sorry, I should have said something earlier, but I hoped... Jenny, Lorna has mental health issues and tonight's obviously not one of her good times. I'll see her and sort things in the morning, but for tonight... I need to sort this out, but not at two in the morning. Grab your overnight gear, you're coming with me.'

'Do you have room?' she asked. She, too, was watching Lorna, realising this wasn't something that could be sorted with a few soothing words.

'I have room,' he said grimly. 'There are reasons...well, my little boy...the dog...'

'I'll keep them apart.'

'I know you will,' he said gratefully. 'There's a bedroom with an en suite at the end of the house we don't use, and the laundry's nearby. Go inside now and grab any gear you need, but do it fast. We both need to sleep and in her current state Lorna isn't going to let anyone sleep here.'

Then he turned to Lorna. 'It's okay, Lorna,' he said, gently though, doctor to patient. 'I'll take Jenny and her dog back to the hospital for the night.'

'Strumpet,' Lorna hissed.

'She's no such thing,' Rob said, his voice still gentle. 'Jenny's a part of our medical team and I think she's just what this town needs.'

CHAPTER FOUR

Jen woke and there was a small child standing in the doorway, looking at her.

Well, so much for keeping boy and dog apart, she thought, and her hand dropped instantly to Stumpy's collar. *Whoops.*

They'd arrived back at the doctor's house after two a.m., silent, both weary almost beyond belief.

'Gary should have warned you,' Rob had told her when they were all back in the car. 'Lorna's been treated for schizophrenia for years—occasionally she needs to be hospitalised. If she stays on medication she can function, but when she comes to me as a patient, I always have a nurse present. If ever a patient's likely to sue me for all I'm worth, it'll be Lorna. She sounds like she's on the edge now—her medication might need to be tweaked.'

Jen had sighed, feeling mortified and more than a bit confused. The studio had seemed perfect.

'When I came for the interview there was a note in the general store advertising the studio,' she'd told him. 'Your local realtor said he could offer no alternative. Lorna seemed pleased to have me as her tenant and I didn't even ask Gary.'

So now she was temporarily homeless—except it seemed she was sharing with Rob, at least for one night.

And Rob's house didn't exactly feel like home. She'd walked into it in the small hours and had been hit by how big it was—and how empty. She'd walked through the cavernous living room to reach the bedroom Rob had suggested and thought it looked like a show home. Rigid furnishings, soulless pictures on the walls, the only personal items being photographs on the living room's marble mantel. There were many photos, all of one person—a young woman.

Rob's wife? The tragedy?

But Rob hadn't paused long enough to explain. He'd carried Stumpy into the laundry. They'd set up a pile of towels on the floor and organised heating so she'd stay warm. Then he'd ushered her to a bedroom—also clinically sterile—and said goodnight.

An hour later Stumpy had started moaning, a low, distressed howl. She'd gone to check and fondled those extraordinary ears—and then Rob had arrived.

He'd been wearing boxers and nothing else. What was it about this man that made her want to gasp?

Pure testosterone, she'd told herself. Any woman would feel it.

'I'm sorry,' she'd told him. 'I didn't want her to wake you.'

'Not your fault,' he'd said and knelt beside her. 'Poor pooch. No dog should go through what she's been through today.'

'I'll take her to my bedroom, if that's okay with you,' she'd told him, almost expecting resistance. She hadn't got it. Instead he'd gathered Stumpy and her bedding against his chest and carried her into Jen's bedroom.

'Can you put her right by the bed where I can touch her?' Jen had asked, and he'd cast her a strange look—a look that was almost puzzled. But he'd obliged, said a simple goodnight and then disappeared. And Jen had drifted back to sleep with her hand dropped down to rest on Stumpy's soft coat.

They'd both slept, woman and dog—and now Rob's son was standing in the doorway. He looked a miniature version of his father. Dark-haired, dark-eyed, his small face serious. He was wearing cute blue pyjamas with dinosaurs

all over them, and he was carrying a battered…
what looked like a toy scarecrow?…by one disreputable leg.

'Why do you have a dog?' he asked.

He hadn't talked to his dad yet?

'Her name's Stumpy,' she told him. 'She was injured last night. Your dad and I bandaged her side and brought her here.'

'Why did you come, too?'

'Someone has to look after Stumpy,' she said, and he thought about it and nodded, gravely accepting.

'My dad's in the clinic, seeing someone who got stood on by a cow,' he told her. 'Minnie's making pancakes. She told me you were here and I wasn't to wake you, but I thought you'd like pancakes.' He took a couple of steps into the room but, before he could go further, Jen was out of bed, crossing to stoop before him, blocking his way.

'Jacob…you are Jacob, aren't you?'

'Yes,' he said, clearly a bit confused at the way she'd deliberately put her body between him and Stumpy. He held out the battered stuffed toy. 'And this is Eric-the-Scarecrow. Minnie says you're Jenny and you drive ambulances. With sirens and everything. And you help Daddy.'

'That's right,' she told him, squatting before

him. 'Jacob, Stumpy isn't very well. We might let her wake up by herself.'

But Stumpy was awake. Her nose poked out from the bundle of towels she'd been lying among, and as she saw Jenny and Jacob her bushy tail gave a tentative wag.

How much did she remember of last night?

Jen had hurt her—she'd had to. Hauling her up the cliff in such a way when her side was so injured must have been excruciating. But there'd been no sign of aggression, no sign of anything except distressed acceptance. And with Jen's hand gently stroking she'd slept in this strange place, with strange people.

Now...that tail lifting in a tentative wag made something inside Jen's heart lurch.

'Can I pat her?' Jacob said. He'd also seen the big ears, the huge brown eyes and the wag of the bushy tail. 'She looks like she'd like a pat.'

But Rob had clearly said... What?

There are reasons...well, my little boy...the dog...'

An allergy? That was the most obvious reason.

'Jacob, sometimes dogs make kids sneeze, a lot. I need to check with your dad that you don't have an allergy before you can pat her. I think we need to go find your Minnie while Stumpy wakes up.'

'Dogs don't make me sneeze,' Jacob said

scornfully. 'Dad says that's an allergy, and my friends Ella and Toby have allergies. Cats and dogs make Ella sneeze all the time, and Toby can't eat peanut butter sandwiches or anything. Dad says I'm very lucky not to have them 'cos they sound pesky. Minnie has a cat at her place and I pat her all the time. Can I pat Stumpy now?'

'We'll see after your dad's checked her,' she temporised. There must be some reason... 'I'll take her out in the garden now—I think she'll need a wee—and then I'll come to the kitchen. Will I meet you there?'

'Me and Eric will watch her have a wee,' Jacob said definitely. 'But we won't touch her. I don't want to hurt her.'

And I don't want to hurt you, Jen thought, deciding, allergy or not, it was totally reasonable for Rob to worry about his kid and a strange dog.

'Okay, will you tell Minnie that I'd really like some pancakes too? Then you can come out to the back veranda and watch, but you're not to come close until your dad says you can.'

'Okay,' Jacob said happily and grinned and left, with Jen thinking... *This kid has a smile just like his father's.*

A gorgeous smile.

A smile to melt hearts?

* * *

There was a pyjama-clad woman and a dog on his back lawn.

Rob had spent an hour coping with a messy foot injury. A decent-sized heifer had stood on Rebecca Ireland's foot, and Rebecca hadn't been dressed for the occasion.

At sixteen, the kid fiercely resented having to work in her parents' dairy. She had to do so every Sunday morning or she'd get no allowance, her parents had told her—they struggled dealing with their large herd alone. But the thought of wearing decent boots had added insult to injury in Rebecca's rebellious teenaged mind. The dry weather meant there was little mud so she'd defiantly worn her trendy new runners. With subsequent consequences.

'It's broken,' she'd sobbed as her mother had helped the limping girl into the hospital clinic. 'And it's all your fault. You shouldn't make me milk.'

Fault. The mere word had made Rob wince, and he'd watched the mum's tired face and seen her flinch before he'd set about fixing the damage.

It wasn't broken but it was bruised, lacerated and filthy.

'Why didn't your boots protect you?' he'd asked, almost conversationally. Then, suspecting he already knew the answer, he added another question. 'Mrs Ireland, why haven't you bought your daughter decent boots?'

'She did,' Rebecca admitted sullenly. 'They're dog ugly and I wouldn't be caught dead in them. Mum finally bought me the trainers I like and now they're ruined.' This was clearly her mother's fault too.

'I guess not wearing boots in the dairy is like not wearing a helmet on a motorbike,' he said, pseudo-sympathetic. 'That messes with your hair—and your image—but people really are caught dead without them. And I do mean dead. You're going to end up with a small scar on your ankle, Rebecca. I'll do my best to make it inconspicuous, but maybe...well, you decide what makes sense in the future.'

'I won't be milking cows in the future.'

'The way I'm seeing it, you might need to.'

He'd cast a glance at her mother—he knew this family well, he knew Rhonda struggled with arthritis as well as the needs of a large family and a dairy farm that brought in an income that was, at best, marginal.

'Your parents are so tired now that they might even need to sell the farm. Your dad told me that a few days back. With no farm, no income... there'd be no money for trendy trainers—there'd be no money for new clothes at all.'

Rebecca's eyes had widened in shock.

'You've seen the kids at school whose parents can't find jobs. How many of them have trendy trainers? You might need to think about it.'

He'd left it there. He'd cleaned, stitched and dressed the foot, but as they'd left Rhonda Ireland had turned and given him a swift hug.

'Thank you,' she'd said, a little bit tearfully, and then her daughter had caught her hand and he'd watched as mother and daughter made their way back to their car.

Thinking…*fault*.

And now… He'd walked out to the back veranda and Jen and Stumpy were on the back lawn and Jacob was watching and he thought of the next word after *fault*.

Consequences.

He thought of Charlie Emerson, an elderly farmer, shy to the point of paranoia, dying of a heart attack. He knew of no relatives, no one to mourn.

But, because of that, on the back lawn was a slip of a girl. She was wearing faded flannel pyjamas. Her hair had been tightly hauled into a knot the night before, but was now cascading to her shoulders as a mass of tangled brown curls. She was tall but slight, or should that be…wiry? Built for service rather than style? That was the sort of comment Emma used to make about herself, he thought, and smiled at the thought. *'I'm a failure,'* she'd wailed. *'Put me in haute couture and everyone'd guess there'd be a khaki chest warmer underneath.'*

Emma. For the thousandth time he demanded of the world: *why won't they let her go?*

And with that thought…consequences. He just knew there'd be consequences of inviting Jenny and Stumpy to stay.

But then Jenny saw him and grinned and waved, and grim thoughts changed to an inexplicable lightness. There was a woman in his backyard in cute pyjamas. There was also a dog, obviously trying to figure the best spot to honour with her ablutions. And Jacob was there, seeing him, squealing in pleasure and bounding along the veranda to join him.

'Daddy, Jenny's got a dog and her name's Stumpy, but Jenny says I can't pat her until you come home. *Please*, Daddy…'

'Pancakes are ready,' Minnie called from the kitchen, and there was another inexplicable shaft of pleasure. And then came the thought…

I've come home.

They ate breakfast together, the cheerful, motherly Minnie supervising, beaming that her pancakes were being appreciated, and joining them at the table so she could boss them to eat more.

Jenny should be dressed, but there'd been no time. She'd taken Stumpy outside fast because…well, when a dog woke from sleep and seemed agitated one couldn't mess around getting dressed. She'd taken her out to the lawn and then Rob had come home and the pancakes were ready…and who was going to waste time dressing when there were pancakes to eat?

And Stumpy…

'I'll take her back to the laundry,' she'd said tentatively, but the dog had whined and rubbed her head against Jenny's pyjama-clad leg and Jacob had looked pleadingly at his dad.

'We could give her a pancake too. Daddy, she wants to be with us, I know she does.'

So the reservations Jenny had heard from Rob the night before seemed to have disappeared. Maybe he'd been worried about the possibility of an aggressive dog, Jenny thought, as she'd watched Rob kneel with his little son and show him just the right way to rub behind Stumpy's soft ears. And Stumpy, wounded, shocked but still dozy and pain-free, courtesy of the drugs Ross had told Rob to give her, had almost purred with pleasure, and as Rob had agreed to let Jacob give her a nibble of plain pancake, the dog's devotion seemed complete.

Stumpy was now lying under Jen's chair, her unwounded side brushing Jen's leg as if she needed the reassurance of touch. But Jacob's chair was just beside Jen's, and his little hand was surreptitiously dropping pancake nibbles to the dog below.

It felt good. No, it felt great.

The night before, Jen's impression of this house was that it was huge and empty. The living room she'd walked through to access her end of the house had looked almost unused. But this room... Well, the kitchen was also large but it was clearly more than a kitchen.

There was a big fire stove at one end—an Aga—set in a cavernous fireplace. At this time of the year it would have heated the room unbearably—Minnie was using a smaller electric hotplate to cook her pancakes—but the Aga gave a sense of age and domesticity that felt good. As did the scrubbed and worn table, the chairs with red gingham cushions and the comfy, faded sofa that took up one end of the room. A small television was mounted on the wall. Books, adult and kids' variety, were scattered on almost every available surface, and an obviously mid-construction building block edifice lay on the rug.

And the kitchen was domestically...muddled? The mantel above the fireplace held a mish-mash of domestic trivia. She could see a kid's attempt at pottery—was that supposed to be a unicorn?

A pile of seashells, some broken. A partial bird's nest, obviously used. A rat trap.

A rat trap?

Rob, sitting opposite, was obviously following her gaze, and as she turned to him he grinned.

'Yep, a rat trap,' he told her. 'Minnie took Jacob to a Father's Day stall at the local market, full of assorted bric-a-brac. Jacob had saved up just enough to afford it and he decided it was the thing I needed most. The lady on the stall helped him gift wrap it with bright blue ribbons. He thinks we might have rats any day now, and it's best to be prepared.'

'Of course it is,' she agreed. 'Great choice, Jacob.'

'I knew Daddy would like it,' Jacob said, pleased, also looking at the mantelpiece. 'And I collected all those shells, and the bird's nest fell out of the tree after all the little birds flew away. And that's my daddy and mummy,' he added.

For, tucked between shells and bird's nest, was a photograph.

She'd seen photographs of this woman before—the living room was full of them. Life-sized portraits, montages of a girl turning to a woman, professional debut and wedding photographs. The living room seemed almost to be a shrine to her memory.

This, though, was different. It was a casual

shot of a couple, a small photograph in a simple wooden frame. Rob and his wife? They'd obviously been hiking—they each had day packs on their backs. They were standing next to a creek, surrounded by trees, the water seemingly rippling along at their feet. The woman was looking up at Rob and laughing and he was smiling, holding her close.

She looked lovely. She looked pregnant.

'I'm in that picture,' Jacob said importantly. 'I'm the bump in Mummy's tummy. Daddy said she patted me all the time when I was in her tummy but she never got to cuddle me when I got out. We feel sad about that.' Then, moving on, 'Daddy, do you have to work this morning or can we take Jenny to the playground? And Stumpy? Stumpy would like the playground.'

'I'm so sorry about your wife,' Jenny said to Rob, because something needed to be said.

'She's still very much a part of who we are,' Rob said simply. 'And I bet if she were here now she'd say, "Get you to a playground."'

And then he hesitated. 'One of us might need to run Stumpy over to Ross in Whale Head later on,' he said, obviously planning his day in his head. 'She'll need antibiotics and I'd like a vet to check her. I talked to Chris earlier—he's having trouble locating anyone related to Charlie so it seems we're the fallback Stumpy carers. But

I just rang Ross, and he's caught up at a tricky calving right now, so we'll let Stumpy sleep for a while. That gives us time to head to the playground.'

He hesitated again, and as if going against his better judgement he added, speaking directly to Jacob, 'But maybe Jenny has other things to do.'

'I need to figure out my housing,' she said. 'But I doubt I can do anything on a Sunday. Would it be okay if Stumpy and I stayed for another night?'

'Yes!' Jacob said, and Minnie beamed as she rose to flip more pancakes.

But then she saw the crease deepen on Rob's forehead. There was a pause, and then he sighed, as if his planning for the day had become even more complicated.

'Sure you can,' he told her. 'Sorry for the hesitation. I was thinking…you'll have so few options.'

'I can go back to Lorna's,' she said doubtfully. 'I've paid a month's rent in advance. It's just… I don't think I can take Stumpy.'

'You can't. Her medication obviously needs adjusting, but even so… There has to be another option.'

She nodded. 'I hope so. But if you can let me stay for another night I'll worry about it tomorrow. Isn't that the best way to approach life?

Never worry about something today which can be equally fretted about in the future. Meanwhile, I'd love to come to the playground. Why not?'

'Why not, indeed?' he replied and gave a rueful smile. 'So, a plan. Pancakes and playground. Does that sound okay to you, Jacob?'

'Yes!' Jacob said, and smiled at his father and then smiled at Jenny, as though including her in some wonderfully exciting scheme.

A walk to a kids' playground? Another night with this man and his little boy?

There was nothing exciting in that at all—was there?

But as she looked across the table and saw Rob's lazy, caressing smile aimed at his small son she thought...yep, there was a reason for the weird tingles she was feeling.

Oh, for heaven's sake... It was hardly more than a month since that appalling night with Darren. But Darren had messed with her life enough, she thought savagely. She was darned if she'd let him mess with...the idea of heading to the playground with a little boy.

And his really gorgeous father.

CHAPTER FIVE

WHY WAS HE thinking this woman—and this dog—could somehow interfere with his life? Surely it was the simplest thing. She needed short-term accommodation and the dog needed short-term care. His house was big, Jenny seemed a cheerful addition, the district needed her skills and there were so few housing options.

Lois and Paul would have kittens.

But his parents-in-law were prone to having… kittens…at a whole lot less provocation than this. Their grief for their daughter had left them almost blinded to everything but the need to preserve her life—and everything and everyone in it. For them, time had stood still since Jacob's birth. Rob's life was supposed to mirror that need.

The path to the beachside park meandered along Willhua Creek. There'd been an unseasonal amount of rain this summer, and the creek was flowing fast enough to make him wary of letting Jacob too close, but the little boy's hand was confidingly tucked into Jenny's. He was giving her a running commentary on the local birds.

'That's a little egret—you can tell 'cos he's smaller and his neck's not bendy. The giant egrets have really bendy necks. And those ones are plovers. They've had their babies now so they don't swoop, but when they're swooping we don't use this path. Their babies are really cute but they're really hard to see. Mum used to take pictures of them—I can show you when we get home if you like.'

He'd been right to bring Jacob back here, he thought, not for the first time. Willhua was their home, and the idea of living in Brisbane, of an indefinite future of mourning, mourning and mourning, was enough to do his head in. It *had* done his head in, and he couldn't allow Jacob to spend any more of his childhood immersed in that grief. Here he was among people who loved him. He was happily surrounded by the sea, the beach, the birds, the nature that Emma loved.

Had loved.

Dear heaven, would they ever allow her to die?

But she *had* died, he told himself, as he'd told himself for four long years, as so many specialist doctors had told him, as they'd also told Lois and Paul.

'There's a Nankeen heron!' Jacob's shout

caused the said Nankeen heron to rise in fright from where it had been wading in the shallows. 'It's still a baby—see its spotty wings? When it's grown up it'll be shiny brown all over. Will I draw you a picture when I get home?'

'Yes, please,' Jen said, watching the heron circle a couple of times, cast them what seemed to be baleful glances and then settle to feed again a little further away. 'I like birds.'

'Me too,' Jacob said, and his hand slipped into hers again and he recounted a silly joke. 'What do you give a sick bird? Tweetment.'

Jenny chuckled and Rob found himself grinning.

They'd found that joke among a stash of kids' books Emma had started building the moment they knew she was pregnant. If only…

Enough.

Today, walking in the sunshine, listening to Jacob's happy chatter, suddenly the need to be free of grief and regret and worry about the weird time-lock he found himself in was almost overwhelming. What harm would there be in asking Jenny to move in with them? Why not?

But then they reached the playground and he saw the long black sedan sliding to a halt in the car park.

'Tony's here,' Jacob said happily, and waved frantically towards the car. 'Hi, Tony!'

There was no response from the car—the tinted windows stayed firmly closed.

'Tony?' Jen asked curiously as Jacob whooped across to the slide.

'Jacob's minder,' he said. 'Or... Lois and Paul's minder.'

She frowned. 'Minder?'

'Courtesy of my in-laws,' he said briefly. 'He's not here all the time but they arrange sporadic checks. They worry about Jacob's level of care. They'd like custody, but there's no way.'

'Of course not,' she said, astounded. 'You're his dad.'

'But they're Emma's parents,' he said simply. 'And I never have been—never will be—good enough for Em.'

There was a moment's pause while she let the preposterousness of this statement sink in—but finally she asked, really, really cautiously, 'Did Emma think you were good enough?'

The question caught him off-balance. He stood still, thinking about it.

He and Emma had met in med school and had been friends from the start. Their social circles, though, were hugely divergent. His mum was single. She worked in their local fish and chip shop, and he'd needed to work there too, every spare hour, to get through medicine. Emma was the only daughter of parents who were wealthy, influential and adoring. They'd been politely tolerant of him when he'd been Emma's friend. When she'd announced she wanted to marry him they'd been appalled.

'She did,' he said softly now, thinking of Emma's reaction to their hostility. 'I remember their questions to me when they objected to us marrying. "What does your mother do for a living? She does *what*? And do you even know who your father is?" Em was furious, gutted by their reaction, but in the end it didn't seem to matter. We were in love, and Emma clearly *did* think I was good enough.'

'Good for her,' Jen said roundly. 'So…they didn't change their minds when they found what an all-round good guy you are?'

He grinned at that, and his mood lightened a little. But still he had to answer the question. 'They never changed their minds. We had a quiet wedding rather than the lavish event Emma said they'd always planned for her. They didn't contribute, but that was okay by us. They came, but they looked like they were attending a funeral. Over the next couple of years we did our best— we threw out olive branches, over and over, but the fact that both of us wanted to practise medicine in the country seemed to them to be the last straw.'

And with that the lightening of his mood

ended. 'Maybe, given time, they would have softened,' he said. 'We certainly hoped so. But then Em fell pregnant, and at thirty-two weeks it all turned to horror.' He stopped, his voice turned bleak.

What had Gary told her? *Bloody tragedy about his wife...*

'Oh, Rob, I'm so, so sorry,' she said softly, sensing the bone-deep pain. 'But surely...' She hesitated. 'Surely they couldn't blame that on you?'

'Of course they could. I wasn't here,' he said heavily. 'It was eight weeks before her due date and I drove to Sydney for the day to listen to an expert discussion on peripheral neuropathy. I left Em gardening, happy, but Minnie popped over mid-afternoon and found her unconscious on the veranda. Eclampsia. The rest...' But he didn't go on. He shrugged and fell into silence.

'So Mummy didn't get to say hello to me,' Jacob interjected. He was sitting on the top of the slide, but he must have had half an ear on what they were saying. Despite the tragedy behind this, he sounded happy, imparting what was obviously a well-known story.

'Gran says she still watches me, all the time. Gran and Grandpa say they can still talk to her, and they send Tony to tell them everything I'm doing so they can tell her. Daddy says maybe she does watch us, and when we have fun then she's happy. We can talk to her here too, in bed at night, when we close our eyes and think about her. Daddy says we don't really need Tony, but Daddy says he makes Gran and Grandpa feel better, so that's okay. He waves to me. Catch me!' he ordered his father, and Rob did.

Jen watched Rob snag his little son in his arms, swing him into his chest and hug, laugh at his delight and then let him go and watch as he ran to the swings.

'I can push myself,' Jacob said importantly as his father stayed beside him. 'You can go away.'

But Rob didn't go far. Jen saw him cast a glance at the black car. There was so much about this situation she didn't understand. It wasn't her business, she told herself, but she was too intrigued not to ask.

'So…the minder?'

'Lois and Paul worry about Jacob,' Rob told her. 'They'd like Jacob to live with them, but Jacob and I think we're fine together.'

'And I don't want to live with Gran and Grandpa,' Jacob said sternly, wiggling onto the swing. 'They cry about Mummy all the time.'

'But surely they have no rights…' Jen started.

'They have rights.' Rob sounded weary, as if this was a conversation he'd had many times before. Changing his mind, Jacob set Eric-the-Scarecrow on the swing and proceeded to swing him high enough to scare the stuffing out of any self-respecting soft toy. Rob watched for a while, and then stepped back a little to stand beside her. Decision made to talk?

'The problem…well, one of the problems when we married was a house, a solid old home in a good part of Sydney,' he told her, his eyes still on Jacob. 'It belongs to Emma's grandmother. Pre Emma meeting me, her grandma made a will, leaving her house to Emma and her brother, Colin. In turn, at their grandma's request, Colin and Emma wrote wills leaving everything to each other. They were both young at the time and it even made sense. Then the old lady was diagnosed with Alzheimer's. She lost the capacity to change her will, but she was still alive when we married—she's alive still.

'But part of Lois and Paul's worry over Em marrying me was around the house. Colin is… well, he has some mental health issues and he struggles. He's living in the house, and he loves it. Em had almost forgotten about the will. But her parents hadn't, or maybe the moment we were married they remembered and panicked. They knew marriage invalidates any previous will.'

'Ouch,' Jen said dubiously, not sure where this was going.

'Okay, long story, but bear with me,' he said. 'Because it turns out it was important. We had lunch with them the day after we were married and they brought it up—if anything happened to Em then Colin would lose the place he loved. Em told them she'd change her will as soon as she got back from our honeymoon, but we were going skiing and we could see they were panicked. And of course Em still wanted Colin to have the house—we both did.

'So they brought out the documents and she signed a codicil saying marriage hadn't invalidated her intentions. It was done in a rush. She had no intention of dying and she thought we could fix things up properly in the future. All we wanted was to get out of there and get on with our honeymoon. And we never realised that what she was signing was not only a will, it was also medical and legal powers of attorney.'

He sighed. 'So that was that, and afterwards… well, to be honest, we forgot about it. Our lives were too full, too happy, to think about changing our wills again, so when Em became…not capable of making decisions herself, her parents took control. They have full power over almost everything.'

'Oh, Rob!' The ramifications of what she was hearing were appalling. 'Oh, no.'

'Their control over Em's medical care when she was so gravely ill was bad enough,' he said grimly. 'But they wanted more—they still want more—and they've used those documents to say they have rights to ongoing influence over Jacob's care.' He sighed. 'In a way...to be honest, their loss has left them unhinged. They have every influential lawyer in the land at their disposal, but so far they haven't been able to win custody. The bottom line is that I'm Jacob's father. They argue though, that I can't be a full-time doctor and take care of Jacob, and they hate that this place is remote. They think I should employ a qualified nanny instead of Minnie—in their ideal world I'd have a staff of nannies on shifts. And then last Easter we had an accident...'

'I got bitten,' Jacob said from behind the swing. 'Wendy O'Hara fell off the slide, right here, and hurt her arm. She was crying and Wendy's mummy was crying too. So Daddy had to take care of Wendy's arm. And Wendy's dog Fred was tied to a tree and he started crying too, so I went over to pat him. And he bit me. But Tony was here and saw from his car and he came over and kicked Fred and broke his leg. Gran and Grandpa say it was Daddy's fault, and Minnie told me that Daddy paid the vet, and Minnie said it was…un…unfair, but Daddy said Fred was just upset 'cos everyone was screaming.'

'Whoa.' There was so much in that statement to unpack. 'So that's why no dogs?' she asked cautiously.

'You got it,' Rob said. 'But you know what I thought this morning?' He was still watching his son, but his voice was suddenly a little unsure. 'I've decided—enough.'

'Enough?' She didn't understand half of this story—surely, as sole parent, Rob's control couldn't be questioned—but standing in the sunshine with this man and this little boy… Maybe she didn't have to understand. Maybe she should just enjoy the sunshine—and the sensation of being…a friend?

'Maybe it's time I drew a line in the sand,' he said.

'Sorry?'

'I imagine you understand how gutted Em's parents are,' he said, sounding as if he was thinking things through as he spoke. 'I've been immersed in my own sadness, but I can still understand theirs. But their demands…the fact that Tony turns up unexpectedly and hovers, just to watch…the fact that they arrive themselves, to visit, unannounced… You've seen the living room—they set that up themselves so Jacob can always see his mum. I've let it be because it was too hard not to. But today…'

He glanced over at the black car. 'Today Tony will report back that I'm here with a woman, and I'm betting that within hours he'll have sniffed out that there's a dog staying at the house as well. They'll be down on me like a ton of bricks.'

He paused but then, slowly and deliberately, he started talking again. 'So here it is. If you can cope with a visit from my in-laws—and I warn you, it won't be pretty—I wonder if you're interested in sharing our house?'

She'd been listening in a certain amount of horror—the idea of in-laws holding such sway seemed inconceivable—and his last statement caught her unawares. 'Sharing?'

'It's a hospital house, so why not?' he said, obviously moving on from in-laws discussion. 'Accommodation in this town is tight but you've seen that our house is huge. We'd need to share the kitchen but nothing else. What's more, because the house is deemed part of the hospital, I pay minimal rent. It's called the doctor's house, but this doctor doesn't need all of it. The hospital board is made up of three sensible locals and they know how much we need a paramedic. I wouldn't be the least surprised if they agreed to your staying and set you a minimum rent as well.'

She frowned, turning it over in her mind. The idea might be good, but there did seem to be complications. Complications she didn't understand, but she glanced across at the black car and winced. 'I won't...cause problems?' she ventured.

'With Paul and Lois? I try very hard to avoid confrontation, but enough. I'm Jacob's father. There needs to be an end to this constant battle.'

'Would having Stumpy make things worse?' Not having to return to Lorna Dumet's was appealing, but this man had obvious issues. And so did she. When she'd settled Stumpy the night before, the dog had raised her soft paw and put it on her arm, and she'd thought...

'Rob, I do like dogs,' she told him. 'And I've sort of fallen for Stumpy. If no relative comes forward to claim her, with her side looking so awful it'll take a month or so for her to look presentable enough for adoption. I've been thinking I'll look after her until that happens, but if I'm to look after her for that time I might...get attached.'

'You think that's a risk?' he asked, bemused.

'I'm not bad at getting attached,' she admitted and then gave a rueful shrug. 'A couple of hopeless exes spring to mind. Stumpy's complications look a doddle in comparison.'

He gave her a curious look. 'So... Stumpy instead of exes?'

'You got it.'

'You're not suffering from a broken heart as well?' he asked, but the way he said it, it wasn't intrusive. It was simply a comment from...a friend?

This man *could* be a friend, she thought, and it was like a frisson of pleasure, bursting through the muddle she'd been in for the last few weeks.

'It's not exactly a broken heart,' she said, knowing suddenly that it was true. In comparison to what he'd gone through, her story was surely nothing. 'Humiliation though. Falling for a toerag.'

'I'm sorry.'

'Yeah, well, yet another life lesson learned. Don't they all come at us when we least need them?' She shrugged and then she gave a wry smile. 'And I did, sort of, leave my mark.'

'What, you bit him, like Fred?'

She chuckled. 'Ugh! Biting toerags would be like voluntarily biting into tripe—not in my life's plan.' But then she paused, thinking of that last night with Darren, the anger, the humiliation, the pain. And then she thought, why not tell someone?

Tell Rob? This man with the smiley eyes? This

man who knew real tragedy, as opposed to her sordid story?

Jacob was busy pushing Eric-the-Scarecrow on the swing. The sun was on her face and there was nowhere to go. If this man was to be her new housemate…why not tell him?

'Darren was my boss,' she said. 'He was hired eighteen months ago to head South Sydney Air Rescue. He had all the qualifications in the world, and the world was his oyster. He was too good-looking for his own good, sexy-as-hell and… Am I boring you?'

'Not at all,' he said faintly, and she grinned.

'Hey, if you're my new housemate, maybe we get to tell each other things. Anyway, he arrived and swept me off my feet, or as much as anyone can sweep someone my height off my feet. He said he'd been married, but things hadn't worked out. She'd taken some bigwig job in New York and their marriage was over. So romance, romance, romance, blah-blah-blah. I won't bore you with the soppy bits. Or how much I made a fool of myself.'

'But then our service was nominated for this huge award, and as its head Darren was due to accept the award at a black tie gala dinner. Politician celebrities, you name it. And of course I was to be his significant other. "Let's make a weekend of it," he said, and I was so excited. I bought the most gorgeous dress. He booked us a suite in the fanciest hotel in Sydney, overlooking the harbour, just dream stuff—and then it all fell apart.'

'Uh-oh.'

She managed a rueful smile. 'Yeah, uh-oh. Idiot me. So come Saturday night, we'd had a lovely lunch, then we'd come back to the room to dress for the presentation dinner. But he got a phone call, and halfway through making ourselves pretty he went outside to take it. And it was his wife. He'd told her about the award and it seemed their marriage wasn't exactly…over. She'd flown back to surprise him, rung from the airport to ask which hotel he was in and she was on her way. And that was that. "I'm married," he said. "And my wife is here. You need to leave."'

'Um…' Rob said mildly. 'Ouch?'

'You could say that,' she muttered. 'Bottom-feeding, two-timing toerag. When he came back to the room after the phone call I was half dressed, and I felt humiliated to my socks—if you could categorise the gorgeous lingerie I'd bought specially for the occasion socks. So I stood there with my mouth open while he said calmly that he'd organised another room for me and changed the dinner seating arrangements. He'd see me at dinner, and would I please remember that we were just acquaintances. After all, he said, it wasn't as if our affair was serious, but now he needed to take a shower. And then he walked into the bathroom and closed the door.'

'Oh, my… I'm so sorry. Jen…'

'Don't be too sorry,' she said, and somehow she managed to smile again. 'You know the saying—don't get mad when you can get even? I stood there staring at the closed bathroom door, and then I stared at his gorgeous bespoke dinner suit laid out on the bed. And my suitcase was on the floor and I'd packed nail scissors.'

'What…you cut it up?' he demanded, appalled, and she chuckled.

'No such thing,' she told him. 'I'm no vandal. I simply…improved it. It was a hot night in Sydney and surely long trousers would be uncomfortable. So I carefully converted them into zigzag-edged shorts, surely much more appropriate than formal attire in the heat. I zigzagged his lovely Italian silk tie to match. Then I packed my stuff and walked out and went home. The next day I started looking for a new job—and here I am.'

'Did he…did you hear what happened?' he asked, horrified but fascinated.

'Of course I did. I gather my friend Frankie had to accept the award on his behalf, because Darren seemed to have come down with a sudden illness. Maybe there was a dearth of dinner suit hire places open at seven on a Saturday night? Anyway, Frankie apparently made a very nice speech and everyone cheered. And thus endeth an affair.'

Only it hadn't ended—at least not like that, though. Not with an insouciant shrug and moving on. There was still enough tension in her voice to tell him the hurt and humiliation had been bone-deep.

He had a sudden urge to find the bastard and do more than rip his pants.

'He's gone back to New York,' she said, watching Eric-the-Scarecrow being swung higher and higher. Her voice was carefully neutral. 'The award was a biggie and it seemed he used it to get himself a great admin job in the States. Head of some city paramedic service where he'll get to sit behind a desk all day. Right up his alley.'

There was a long silence. Eric-the-Scarecrow fell off the swing a couple of times and was retrieved and sent sky-high again. *Get up and move on*, Jen had told herself that first morning, when all she'd wanted to do was move on. And she had.

'So it seems to me,' Rob said at last, cautiously, into the stillness, 'that we're both in the mood for moving on.'

And there was only one answer to that.

'Indeed I am. Why on earth not? Housemates?

Dog? Onward and upward, I say.' She glanced at Jacob, who'd suddenly abandoned Eric and was clambering up a chain tepee. 'Jacob, do you mind if I join you at the top?'

'Will you come up?' Jacob said, sounding startled. 'It's very high.'

'But I'm good at climbing,' she told him. 'Very good. So maybe it's time I climbed right out of the funk I've been in and come up to join you.'

Frankie rang that afternoon, while she was moving her stuff out of Lorna's to Rob's. Because, just like that, she now had a new home.

Of course she was copping invective from Lorna and sacrificing two weeks rent, but she'd be living with Jacob and Rob. Friends? Surely they could be. There was also the possibility of keeping a very nice dog.

And…a guy who made her smile? Whose own smile made her…

'Hey!' Frankie's voice down the line was welcome—they'd been friends for a long time. 'How goes it?'

She'd just finished stowing boxes into her car. She stopped and leaned on the bonnet and felt the sun on her face. The smell of the sea was everywhere, plus the eucalyptus from the giant gums overhead. Three blocks away was her new home. With Stumpy and Jacob. And a very nice man called Rob.

'It goes pretty well,' she told Frankie and filled her in.

'Um,' Frankie said at last as she finished. 'Jen?' And Jen heard doubt.

'What?'

'Can I remind you how fast you fell for Darren?'

'I'm not falling,' she said hotly. 'I'm just… He could be a friend, that's all. Stumpy's messy but she's recovering. We haven't found any relations yet, but there's still time. If no one comes forward though, I might just adopt her myself. So tell me about Bruce.'

'He's okay,' Frankie said, abandoning the inquisition. 'He's got a bruised leg that's been all bandaged up by the vet, but nothing's broken. I'll let Nico know that you haven't found any relatives.' There was a huff of laughter from Frankie. 'He might be happy about that. I think they quite like each other. Like you and Stumpy.' Then there was a sigh. 'Just be careful, won't you? Falling for a dog…falling for a man…'

'I'm not falling for a man.'

'No, twenty-four hours isn't long enough to fall for anyone,' Frankie said darkly. 'Neither, in my opinion, is falling a good idea at all. Do your homework, my friend, so you don't end up getting a nasty surprise down the track. You know as well as I do that if they want something from you, they can hide stuff you should know about. Like a wife. Or a new, better girlfriend? Just remember that.'

'I'll remember,' she said and disconnected and tried for a whole five minutes to feel sober and reflective and careful.

And then she thought of Rob and Jacob and Stumpy and her new job and her new life—and she decided she didn't need to feel sober and reflective and careful at all.

CHAPTER SIX

WHAT FOLLOWED WERE a couple of weeks where Jenny decided the job of paramedic at Willhua could well turn out to be a very fine career choice. She loved it.

The service was busy, but not usually with casualties. The main medical service for the district was at Whale Head, and infirm patients without their own transport options needed to be ferried back and forth.

The service's second vehicle was a minibus. One of the retired locals was the usual driver, but for that first week Harold was down with a heavy cold and Jen had to step in. She'd been dubious, but the end of the week, instead of feeling like a glorified taxi service, she was starting to realise what a great little community this was.

Sam Dutton was going back and forth for kidney dialysis. Marianne Carmichael was halfway through radiotherapy for breast cancer. Timmy Loden, six years old, had lost a leg to sarcoma and needed to visit Whale Head twice a week for rehabilitation physiotherapy. They were a motley set of patients, but somehow they gelled.

Timmy's parents were passionate surfers, and their shock was still palpable months after their son's surgery. The elderly Sam was an ex-surfer as well, so there was stuff to talk about—but Timmy's missing leg made initial conversations constrained.

The second time Jenny drove the truck, though, Sam produced photos of a mate of his who'd lost his leg to a shark some twenty years ago and was surfing still. Sam had pictures of his mate surfing one-legged—he even had pictures of the shark! Marianne oohed and ahhed, then borrowed the pictures, enlarged them overnight and the next day brought the essentials for Jen to stick them up in the truck.

'You want me to draw teeth marks on your stump?' Sam had asked. The next trip Marianne had produced indelible markers and the teeth marks looked…real enough for Timmy to love them.

The power of community in the little truck seemed almost breathtaking, Jenny thought, and this power extended beyond the patients they were transferring.

'You're staying with Doc Pierson?' she was asked, over and over. She was looked over with interest, but again there was warmth. The common consensus? 'Well, that's wonderful. They rattle around in that great big house. You'll look after them, won't you, love?'

But right now *they* seemed to be looking after her.

There'd been an emotional call from Charlie Emerson's daughter, still reeling from the loss of her dad. 'I'm so sorry, but I can't take the dogs. I live in an apartment in Sydney. When I sell the farm I might be able to buy something bigger, but that'll take ages. Besides, I really like my apartment. Is there anyone who can take them?'

Jen still wasn't sure what the fate of the dog Frankie had rescued—Bruce—would be but she knew he was being well looked after for the moment, and she had enough support from Rob and Jacob to give her own promises.

'Stumpy's safe with me,' she'd promised. The dog's side was healing. She still looked appalling, with little hair and scabbing on the left side of her body, but her personality was already showing. She was gentle, inquisitive, answering to her name, sitting when requested—and when Jacob surreptitiously offered her toast crusts she practically turned herself inside out in a display of gratitude that made them all laugh.

And they did laugh. The arrangement was

supposed to be independent living but that had lasted a whole two minutes. With Stumpy at one end of the house and Jacob at the other…yeah, well…

'This house is starting to feel like home again,' Minnie said in satisfaction after the first week. 'You and your blessed dog seem like magic.'

Jen and her dog seemed to have transformed his life. Just like that. One slip of a girl—okay, maybe slip was the wrong word, she was almost as tall as he was, but she was slim, lithe, tanned and fit. Wearing her paramedic uniform she looked ready to face down the world, and that was what she seemed to have done for his world. She giggled at Jacob's corny jokes, she admired his weird artwork and she kicked the footy round the backyard with him. She sat with him on the back veranda with Stumpy between them, gently teaching Jacob how to stroke behind those big soft ears to give Stumpy maximum pleasure.

And she gave *him* pleasure. For the first time since, well, since Emma, the house seemed to be alive again.

She was an appalling cook—she admitted that. 'There's nothing wrong with egg on toast and an apple,' she'd told an appalled Minnie.

Minnie cooked the basics for them when Rob was busy, but he'd always enjoyed cooking. There'd seemed little impetus, though, when it was just himself and Jacob, and Jacob thought pasta, pasta and pasta—with the occasional hit of sausages—was all a four-year-old required.

But with Jen here—when the afternoon ended early enough—he found himself hauling out cookbooks that had been ignored for years, and heading into the supermarket on his way to and from house calls to check out the 'international' shelves.

His triumph so far had been his *Chiles en nogada*. Jacob had refused it on the grounds that, 'It has ingredients! Yuk!' They'd given him spaghetti instead, but Jen had raved. He'd gone to bed that night feeling smug and light and... happy.

One woman, one dog, two weeks...

He was due to take Jacob to Brisbane this weekend—the agreement was once a month—and no doubt that'd bring the fog back again, but for now...

For now things seemed okay. The way Jen made him smile...the way he felt when he looked at her hugging her disreputable dog...the way she made his little son chuckle...

He wouldn't look into the future. For now... well, for now things seemed great.

* * *

Thursday night—or was it Friday morning?—
Jen's phone buzzed into life and she was instantly awake. That was what medical training
did for you—there was never any time to yawn
and stretch and bring yourself back to consciousness with ease.

'Jen?' It was Gary. 'Call. Pick you up in three
minutes? I'm ringing Doc now to expect us.'

Even after only two weeks they had this down
to a fine art.

She didn't ask more—the tone of Gary's voice
said there was urgency and he could fill her in on
the way. Three minutes later she was uniformed
and heading for the back door. Rob was already
awake, dressed and in the kitchen.

'Teenager,' he said briefly, 'Anna Windsor.
Gary says sounds like appendix, but her parents are panicking. If you decide to take her on
to Whale Head pick me up on the way. I'll contact Minnie.'

She nodded and left him, heading out into the
dark to wait by the kerb for the flashing light of
the ambulance.

She slid into the seat beside Gary and saw his
face was set.

'What are we facing?'

'Hysterical parents first off,' he said as he hit
lights and sirens. Willhua's tight cliff roads made

it almost essential to give as much warning as they could to oncoming traffic.

'Anna's eighteen. She went to bed without eating, saying she had a tummy upset. Now she's curled up in bed, her parents say she's screaming with pain but she won't let them near. She's yelling at them to get out every time they go near. Heaven knows why. Her mum's bleating appendicitis but, by the sound of it, blocked bowel? Gallstones? Your guess is as good as mine.'

'Tell me about the family.' They had time before arrival, and if they were faced with hysterical parents, background could help.

'They're do-gooders,' he said, in a voice that wasn't exactly full of admiration. 'In the worst possible way. Marjorie and Graham Windsor think their role is to keep the town nice. They run the local pharmacy, Windsor and Son—it's been in the town for generations. Graham considers himself pretty much Willhua's founding father, and Marjorie concurs. If one stray tumbleweed wanders down the main street they'll be out looking for the source, and woe betide the owner of the garden they think it comes from.'

As a character description it took some beating. Jen gave a wry smile. 'And their daughter?'

'Anna. Only child. Nice kid, clever they say, but incredibly quiet. Kept on a tight rein. They've been telling the town she's going to be a doctor since she was seven. Imagine if she decides to be an accountant. Oh, the shame.'

She chuckled at that, and then settled, putting herself into the quiet zone she tried to move into before she faced a job.

Two minutes later they were at the front door. The house and garden were almost rigidly perfect, the brass bell-pull at the front door so shiny it hardly needed the outside light.

But as they approached a scream split the night, a scream so primeval, so full of pain that Gary opened the front door without knocking. Her parents, Marjorie and Graham, were outside a bedroom door, Graham looking wild-eyed and desperate, Marjorie crouched on the floor, holding her knees as if she herself was in pain.

'She won't let us in,' Graham said hoarsely. 'Marjorie tried, she went in but Anna screamed even louder and told her to get out or she'd kill herself. My Anna. My little girl.'

Gary and Jen exchanged glances. They were both experienced paramedics. They'd both been in situations where parents were the last thing a kid needed. Drug use? Alcoholic poisoning? The one that sprang to mind now though—they'd both heard that primeval scream—was also one they'd both faced before.

'By the sound of that pain she'll need hospital,' Gary said firmly.

'But what…?' Marjorie said wildly. 'What…?'

'Possibly a kinked bowel. Possibly gallstones. Doc will examine her.'

'She won't let you in.'

Gary nodded to Jen. If what they were both thinking was right…

'Let Jen try,' he suggested. 'She's nearest to Anna's age. Sometimes pain makes you feel like a trapped animal—weirdly, a complete stranger might be more effective.'

And, before they could answer, Jen slipped quietly into the room.

The room was pink. Very pink. Fifty shades of pink? Pink pile carpet, pink curtains, a pink four-poster bed. A huge desk under the window was piled with impressive texts. A girl was crouched almost in a foetal position under the pink duvet.

The squirrel-shaped bedside lamp cast the only light. Jen hesitated, then went and crouched by the bed, finding the girl's hand. The thin hand she found gripped like death. Then came another scream, this time muffled. Fingernails dug in so hard Jen would later find scratches. The foetal position changed to arching. Pressure, pressure, pressure…

And then the pressure eased. The girl looked wild-eyed at Jenny—and then she folded back into herself.

'Don't tell. Don't tell!' she whispered.

Gary had slipped in behind her. Jen looked back at Gary—and their shared look said they were both guessing what this was about.

'Anna, I'm Jenny and I'm an ambulance officer,' Jen said gently as she bent close to the girl's head. 'You can't cope with this pain alone. Gary and I are here to take you to hospital. Doc Pierson—you know Doc Pierson?—he's waiting for you, but I need to check your tummy first. Will you let me?'

There was a wild nod—the girl was obviously too far gone to argue. 'But not…not Mum and Dad,' she managed.

'That's your choice,' Jen said, still gently. 'But we can talk about that later. Your mum and dad are staying outside while we help you. Now, I'm going to feel your tummy.'

Gary moved silently into position and helped her move the bedclothes from the girl's convulsive, covering grip. Even through the bedclothes they could feel the hard swell of her tummy. She lay limp while Jen did a fast examination.

Suspicion confirmed. A baby. Coming soon.

Another contraction. Another terrified grip and muffled scream.

'Anna, do you know your baby's coming?' Jen asked, as Gary moved to the side of the room and spoke softly into the radio. It seemed impossible the girl didn't know, but terror could sometimes make it possible to block out the most obvious of pregnancies.

'Of course I know,' Anna sobbed. 'But I can't…'

'You can,' Jen told her. 'Your body's doing exactly what it needs to be doing—and you have the strength to help it. Do you know…' She hesitated at this, not sure if it was right to push the girl further, but it was important information. And Gary had said this girl was bright. 'Anna, do you know how long you've been pregnant?'

'Thirty…thirty-seven weeks,' Anna moaned. 'But I can't…'

'You can,' Jen said again, more strongly. 'You're a strong, capable woman, Anna, and you now have all the help you need.'

'But Mum and Dad…'

'We'll be with you when you tell them,' she told her. 'You're not alone any more, Anna.'

Okay. Enough talking. It was time to get her to hospital. Time to bring Rob and his skills into this scenario—and Jen suspected it'd be more than medical skills that were needed tonight.

'Anna, first things first. We need to get you to hospital. Doc Pierson is waiting.' She thought, not for the first time, how awesome was the responsibility facing family doctors. Rob would be facing more than just a simple birth tonight.

'For now let's get you shifted to where we can ease the pain and help you with what's to come.'

Rob was waiting at the hospital entrance. Minnie was already installed in the house. Gary had briefed him while driving—it seemed Jen was in the back with Anna.

'I can't imagine how she's hidden it,' Gary had told him. 'From the whole town? I've seen her myself, walking to and from school. I thought she was putting on weight, but she's been wearing T-shirts about three sizes too big. Well, they all are, seems it's the latest thing, baggy, baggy, baggy. But how her parents didn't know... Or maybe they did, in a way. I'm thinking it must be that thing, you know, where the mind can't take in the bleeding obvious because it's too big. Anyway, when her mum tried to get in the truck with us Anna started screeching again, said, "Stay with Dad, stay with Dad." So they're coming behind, but fair go, Doc, you have a right drama to face.'

So by the time the ambulance doors were opened and Jen emerged, seamlessly helping Gary move the stretcher and roll it into their small theatre, he'd pretty much prepared himself for hysterics to come.

But not from Anna. The moment the stretcher's wheels were down and Jen could be at her side again, the girl's hands clutched hers, but she seemed to be in as much control as a woman nearing her time could be.

'Jen says you won't tell Mum and Dad…unless you have to… I mean…'

'Anna, you're eighteen, an adult. I need your permission for anything I talk to your mum and dad about,' he told her. Then he turned to the night nurse. 'Cathy, could you deflect Mr and Mrs Windsor? Ask Kita to make them a cup of tea. Put them in my consulting room—it's the furthest from Theatre so they won't hear as much. Then I'll need you in Theatre. You too, Jen, if you'll stay.'

He wanted Jen as well as Cathy. Kita was the backup night staff, with basic training only, and she wasn't much older than Anna. Possibly not mature enough to hide her shock.

'I don't think you'll disengage Jen anyway,' Gary said dispassionately, looking at the death grip on Jen's hand.

'Another contraction,' Jen said. 'That's less than two minutes. It's okay, Anna, grip as hard as you like, harder if you want. Someone's looking after Mum and Dad. Now, we need to look after you.'

'They'll guess,' Anna whispered. 'They'll kill me. I can't…'

'Yes, you can.' Rob took her other hand as

the contraction eased. He knew this girl. He'd treated her for acne, for menstrual pain, for a consultation eight months ago when her mother had brought her to him for 'depression'. She'd said sullenly that it was just drama at school, but it was sorted and she didn't need help. He hadn't been able to take it any further but, thank heaven, he hadn't prescribed the antidepressants her mother had insisted she needed.

'You're a strong woman, Anna Windsor, and strong women rule the world,' he told her. 'Isn't that right, Jen? Jen's our newest ambulance officer and you know what she did on her first day here? She abseiled down Devil's Pass to save a life. She even managed to climb up, holding a full-sized corgi. If she can do that, you can push out a baby.'

'I can't…'

'You can,' Rob said again, softly but with total authority in his voice. 'You're not alone now, Anna. With our help, you will.'

'You won't leave me?' But the girl was talking to Jen.

'We're with you all the way,' Jen told her, because there was nothing else to say. She was thinking of what this girl had endured—months of fear, months of hiding what to her must have been a terrifying secret. 'What Dr Pierson says is the truth. Now, during the birth and afterwards, we promise that you won't be alone again.'

Which was how, for the next two hours, Jen found herself acting as a birth partner.

Medically she wasn't needed. Cathy and Rob did everything they could to ease the pain, to ease the panic, to ease the terror. She simply sat and let Anna grip her hand as much as she needed. She wiped her face with a damp towel, which sometimes Anna wanted, though sometimes her hand was slapped away. She listened to swearwords, to curses, to pleas, to rants directed at someone called Tyler, to cries for her mother, but desperate pleas saying no when Cathy offered to fetch her.

And, through it all, Rob's gentle voice. 'You're doing great, Anna. I know it hurts like hell but it'll soon be over. Breathe through the mask— Cathy's holding it for you. You can do this. I know how strong you are…'

Most doctors would disappear at this stage, Jen thought, leaving the waiting for the midwives. There was no urgent need for him to stay—Cathy could call him back at the end. But Anna's eyes kept flying to him as she surfaced from each contraction, and Jen knew that his presence was important. Rob was her family doctor. She knew him. Jen and maybe Cathy as well were strangers. Even though it was Jen's hand the girl was gripping as if she were drowning, Rob seemed her anchor.

And he made a great anchor, Jen decided as the labour progressed. Big, solid, infinitely reassuring, he was the teenaged mum's rock, her link to her parents—her link to reality?

And when that final push came, when a tiny, mewling baby finally emerged into the glare of the overhead lights, when Cathy lifted the little boy onto his mother's breast and Anna sobbed and cradled her baby and looked up, she looked to Rob. Her eyes were filled with tears and fear—but also wonder.

'He's mine,' she whispered, and unconsciously her hands tightened around her little one. 'They'll kick me out. They'll kill me, but he's mine.'

'He is yours,' Rob said infinitely gently as Cathy took over midwife duty—cleaning away the afterbirth, the detritus of the last two hours. He sat on the bed beside Anna and used his finger to trace a feather touch on the tiny downy cheek. 'Your son.' And then his voice softened. 'Anna, your mum and dad are going crazy with worry out there. What would you like me to tell them?'

'Tell them to go home.'

There was a long silence at that. Jen thought she should go home too—surely she was no longer needed—but the moment she walked out of this door she'd have to walk past the room where the Windsors waited. What would she say? Whoever walked out of this room first had to have their ducks in a row. To walk out and say nothing—impossible.

And Rob knew it. This whole situation was impossible. The best thing for Anna now was to be left in peace with her baby, with Cathy in the background to help, if help was needed. But how possible was that?

As a paramedic Jen had been present at births before—they usually got their mums to hospital in time, but she'd seen babies born at home, babies born in the ambulance, once even a baby born on the side of the road before the ambulance reached them. But in every single case there'd been someone. A partner, a mother, a sister, a friend. Someone to hold and love and share the awe. This frightened child—for that was what she seemed—appeared to have no one.

'Have you told anyone?' Rob asked gently, and Anna shook her head.

'One night. And he's not even my boyfriend. The school dance. We got together beforehand, us girls, and Georgie Lewis had vodka. We drank it with cola. Dare, she said, and we all did, or at least I thought we all did, but maybe she put more in mine. And then Tyler...' Her eyes filled. 'He'd been nice to me but it was a dare. I don't…please…don't even say his name. I'm the goody two-shoes at school and the next day…they were all pointing and laughing—Tyler must have given Georgie the vodka. It was a set-up. He was dancing with me and he's so popular, so good-looking… I remember feeling dizzy and great and like I was one of them! But I wasn't. Then we sneaked out and it was only the once and I couldn't… I didn't…'

And Jen saw Rob's face darken. He'd know these kids. He'd be seeing the whole picture, she thought. An overly protected kid, a *goody two-shoes.*

'That's enough,' Rob said, infinitely gently now. 'That's past, done with. There'll be ways we can sort out what needs to be sorted out with Tyler, but for now all that's important is you and your little boy. Anna…'

'I want to keep him.' Her eyes, desolate while telling her appalling story, suddenly flashed fire. Her arms tightened on her little one. 'I was so scared and then he started moving inside me and I could feel him and I knew… I knew I'd feel like this. He's mine. He's nothing to do with Tyler, nothing to do with my parents. But I don't know…'

'You don't need to know,' Rob told her. He

was still sitting on the side of the bed, his finger was still stroking the tiny baby's cheek.

'You know, Anna, my mum was seventeen when she had me. She was just like you, a scared kid, but she knew what she wanted. She wanted me. And somehow she managed. Her parents weren't there for her, but someone at the hospital was. Someone helped her to find somewhere to live, how to get government help. She and I had fun—she was a great mother. She died of cancer two years ago, but she told me, over and over, the two biggest things she learned. The first was to face down those who judged her— she was proud of herself and she was proud of me. The second was to ask for help when she needed it. So what's happened in the past…it was no fault of yours, Anna, but what's come out of it is something wonderful. Something you can be proud of forever. Your son.'

And the girl's gaze, drowning in the wonder of her baby, moved up to his. 'I can do that?'

'If you want, you can do anything. There are people who can help you. I can help you and Cathy can help you. We can hook you up with services that'll keep you and your baby safe. But first…' He hesitated and then went on.

'Outside, your parents are going out of their minds with worry. They've probably guessed what's happening—or maybe Gary was forced to tell them. Once upon a time they looked down at you just like you're looking at this little one. Will you let them come in and see you?'

There was a flash of terror at that, and then she closed her eyes and when she opened them again something had changed.

'You said,' she whispered, but there was a subtle difference in her voice now, the determination to move forward. 'You said…to ask for help when I need it.'

'I did say that and I meant it.'

'Could you…' She hesitated. 'It's just… I've been trying for all this time and I can't… Can you tell them about the vodka and the dance and…and what happened? Only not names, please not names. I don't want…'

'You don't want anger tonight,' Rob said and smiled and snagged a couple of tissues from the bedside table and wiped her eyes. 'Of course you don't. Tonight is your son's birthday. It's a day of joy and wonder and welcome.'

'And you'll come in when they come? You won't leave me alone until…'

'I'll stay as long as you need me.'

'So will I,' Cathy said roundly. 'Anyone upsetting my patients tonight will have me to answer to.'

'But I need to go home,' Jen said simply. Her place was no longer here; Cathy and Rob were all the girl needed. She'd backed away from the bed, leaving the tableau to doctor, nurse, mother and baby. 'Congratulations, Anna. You did magnificently and I know you'll keep on doing the same.'

'But…you helped me.'

'I'll come back to see you tomorrow,' Jen told her, 'I promise. You're calling the shots now, Anna. We're all here to help, for whatever and however long you need.'

CHAPTER SEVEN

ROB FOUND JEN an hour later, in the laundry.

For four years Rob had been accustomed to nights of solitude, of reheating dinners Minnie had left for him, sitting in the darkened kitchen/family room—because who'd want to go into that mausoleum of a living room?—and staring at nothing until tiredness overcame him.

Minnie would still be here—she had a room next door to Jacob's that she slept in on nights like this. The slightest sound from Jacob would have her springing up in full childcaring mode, but she was so used to Rob coming and going that his movements didn't disturb her. Jen's room was at the far end of the house. He assumed she'd be long asleep as well, so the night was his, the demons to be faced alone.

He washed, he headed into the kitchen and flicked the kettle on—and then he heard a voice—Jen's voice—coming from the laundry. Soft and gentle, a murmur only.

'You're doing great, Stumpy. I know I woke you up, but you can go to sleep again now. And I know you're missing Charlie and Bruce, and your side still hurts, but we'll figure a way to get you through that. You and me together. Friends for life. How does that sound?'

It sounded okay to him. He headed to the laundry and stood in the doorway and watched.

She didn't see him at first. She was wearing pyjamas and sitting on the floor, legs out in front, Stumpy's boofy head on her knee. She was stroking her over-big ears, still murmuring.

'Tomorrow I reckon we might dawdle down to the park, not fast, not far, just far enough to find a few interesting smells. Rob and Jacob say lots of dogs go to the park, so there'll be great smells all over the place. Maybe we might even make a doggy friend or two.'

She bent and gave the dog a kiss on the head and then lifted her back onto her pile of bedding. The dog looked adoringly up and then nuzzled back into the soft wool.

Was this a nightly occurrence, chatting to Stumpy in the small hours? The way Stumpy was settling, he suspected it was.

This woman... He thought about the way she'd responded to Anna over the past few hours, the way she'd sat and let the girl cling, the soft things she'd said to her. 'I'll come back to see you tomorrow,' she'd said as she'd finally left. 'I promise.'

This was a woman who kept her promises.

This was a woman who made his heart twist.

But now she was looking up, seeing him. There was no start of astonishment though, just a warm smile, as if he was simply a part of her world. And right now it felt like that was the way it was. Her flannel pyjamas were oversized, and her dark curls were tousled—she usually had them pulled back but now they drifted to her shoulders. Her face looked scrubbed. She was obviously ready for bed.

So why did he say, 'Hey, well done on settling your patient. I'm making tea and toast. You want to share?'

'I did have tea with Minnie when I got home,' she confessed and then she beamed. 'But drama makes me hungry and I could definitely use more.'

Uh-oh. What was she saying?

This was not sensible—not sensible in the least. There was no need at all for her to stay with Rob for a moment longer. She was this man's tenant and a colleague, and that was all. She lived at the far end of the house. She needed to keep some distance.

But distance had never been Jen's strong suit.

Maybe it was her childhood, absent parents who'd appeared sporadically, causing her to cling fiercely, to take what she could because she'd known they wouldn't be there the next day.

Maybe that was why she'd jumped into all sorts of disastrous relationships—okay, Darren hadn't been the first. Jump first, ask questions later. Take people at face value because looking forward didn't change a thing.

And here it was, happening again. This man had so much baggage—impossible baggage—yet here he was, looking down at her, smiling, and here was that longing again—for closeness, for warmth, for connection.

Her friend Frankie might have poured a bucket of cold water over her, she thought, demanding, 'Will you ever learn?' But right now...

Right now Rob was reaching down to help her up. His hands were strong and warm, and his smile was oh, so lovely.

Maybe this time...

What was she thinking? It was too soon—way, way too soon.

But that smile... She had no hope of fighting the way his smile made her feel.

And he tugged her a little too strongly, or maybe she rose a little too fast, and all of a sudden she was very, very close.

Here comes another catastrophe! She could almost hear Frankie's inevitable warning.

But Rob was right here, and she could feel his warmth, his strength... His lovely hands were steadying her, and he was still smiling.

She was lost.

Here I go again.

She could hear her brain almost sighing in exasperation, but did she care?

Not tonight. Not when he was so close.

So, she thought blindly as she felt the warmth of his chest, felt his hands steady her. Catastrophe, here I come.

This felt risky. Really, really risky.

Why risky? Wrong word. If not risky then what was the word for the way he was feeling?

There was no one word, he decided. Meanwhile, he needed to release her, but just for a moment his steadying turned to something more.

What?

Suddenly it felt as if his world was changing. Doors that had slammed shut four years ago were suddenly inching open.

But nothing was said. There was a loaded silence as finally his hands dropped away. There was silence as they moved to the kitchen, put the kettle on, concentrated on the minutiae of toast-making. Settled at the kitchen table as if nothing was between them.

He should make this fast and head to bed, he told himself, fighting to escape sensations he wasn't sure how to deal with. Sensations he had no right to be feeling. Tomorrow would be a heavy day. The repercussions of tonight's baby were going to be far-reaching—and he and Jacob were due to fly to Brisbane in the evening.

Brisbane. The thought made his heart sink. Over and over, they made the journey, with Jacob objecting every step of the way.

'I don't like them crying,' he'd say. 'I don't want to stay in that room any more.'

Neither did he. The thought of his lovely Emma...

No. He wouldn't think of that tonight. He couldn't, because emotions seemed to be heightening by the minute.

Right now he was sitting across the kitchen table, sharing tea and toast with a woman who almost seemed to glow with life. Who made him feel...alive.

She'd been superb tonight. A trained midwife could hardly have done better. That level of support for a woman in labour was surely not in her training, yet she'd stayed, unasked, and he'd felt Anna taking strength from her presence.

'So what's happening next door?' she queried, coming back to the prosaic as she watched him butter her toast. 'More,' she added. 'There's a school of thought that says you should butter your toast lavishly while it's hot, wait until it all melts and then put another butter layer on top. I like that school of thought. Oh, and peanut butter on top of that, please.'

'You're kidding.'

'I would never kid about anything as serious as toast.' She'd made tea and brought mugs to the table, then sat and watched as he followed her toast recipe. Her first bite seemed pure sensual pleasure. 'What?' she demanded. 'You've never watched a woman eat toast before?'

He grinned, but suddenly, through all the other sensations crowding in, there was a jab of memory. Emma. She'd never have layered toast like this—she'd been too health-conscious. A lot of good that had done, though.

'What?' Jen said suddenly. 'What did I say?'

'Nothing.'

'It's your wife, isn't it?' Her voice became gentle. 'You must miss her so much.'

'Four years is a long time.'

'I don't think counting's helpful,' she said, still gently. 'Missing is just…missing.' She watched him for a moment and then obviously decided to return to the events of the night. As a way of alleviating the tension?

'So the Windsors now have a grandson? How did they take the news?'

'Like stunned mullet,' he told her. 'But in a way, subconsciously, maybe they already knew. She's been withdrawn, wearing baggier and baggier clothing, spending time with her books and not her friends. Maybe pregnancy was something they couldn't bear to face, couldn't possibly confront her with. But when you left, when Master Windsor decided he liked his mother's milk, when Anna was almost euphoric with post baby bliss—plus the lingering effectiveness of the drugs—we talked and decided there'd be no better time to bring them into the equation.'

'Primed?' she queried, but sounding like she already knew the answer. 'You talked to them first?'

'Of course. Just to tell them the outline of what she'd told us—she gave me permission. I told them that "How?" didn't come into the equation tonight, and also that I'd promised to stay. The moment I sensed any distress then I'd call a halt.'

'Kick them out, you mean.'

'If I needed to.' He gave a half smile. 'But in the end I didn't. At first they were so shocked they could hardly speak. I could practically see Marjorie summoning the force of her judgemental ancestors as she headed in, but then she saw Anna, she saw the distress—and then she saw the baby.'

'She folded?'

'She just crumpled,' he said in satisfaction. 'I'd forgotten Marjorie's patient history—two still-born babies. She looked down at the little one, and then she looked at her own Anna. I could almost see the moment she remembered that this girl was her own baby—and then she started to cry. And the moment she did, Graham caved as well. He, too, crumpled at the sight of the baby in his daughter's arms, and when I left he was muttering, "A son, my Anna has a son!" I could practically see him in the main street tomorrow, up a ladder, repainting the Windsor and Son sign on his shopfront. Tomorrow I suspect they'll also find out all about Tyler. Anger will kick in, but I suspect that anger won't be directed at Anna.'

'You mean, all that secrecy for nothing?'

'Not for nothing.' He'd been thinking it through as he'd watched them. 'If Anna had announced she was pregnant early on, I'm pretty sure their puritanical instincts might have meant anything could have happened. But now…'

'Now they're learning some instincts are stronger than others.' She beamed. 'Yay for instincts.' She rose to carry her plate to the sink. He rose as well, a bit too fast. She swerved a little and caught her foot on the leg of the chair. He reached out to steady her.

And then let her go?

Well, that was what he should have done. That was what any sane, right-minded male would have…

Um…not. Any sane, right-minded male right here, in the small hours, looking down at this lovely pyjama-clad girl, might have frozen. As he did. His hand stayed on her arm and she looked at it, as if questioning.

And back came all those emotions, all those sensations—or maybe they'd never gone away, just been suppressed.

How long had emotion been suppressed?

She was looking up into his face and, amazingly, she was smiling. Almost laughing.

'Instincts,' she said again. 'They get in the way all the time. Or maybe they don't get in the way. Maybe they just tell us when we're right. Did you know that you're a very nice man, Dr Pierson?' There was a moment's pause and then she said, 'Did you know that right now, also, you're amazingly, astonishingly sexy?'

The room seemed to hush. The whole world seemed to hush. There was a long, long silence while they stood, with his hand on her arm, while she smiled up at him, her teasing smile fading to a slight question.

And then she seemed to collect herself, lifting her arm away, dodging so she could put her plate in the sink. 'Just saying,' she said, almost airily, but there was a sense of breathlessness about her. 'My instincts right now mean I'm probably risking all sorts of rental agreements and putting housemate status at risk. But...'

'But it's only weeks since...'

'Since the Greatest Zigzagged Dinner Suit Incident of the Century? I know.' She had her back to him now, rinsing her plate, even though it surely didn't need rinsing when it was headed for the dishwasher. 'I should still be a soggy heap of humiliation, but somehow I'm getting it in perspective. Or maybe this isn't perspective, the way I'm feeling.' She took a deep breath and turned back to him. 'It's just...this night, the way I'm feeling... You, Rob Pierson, are one amazingly sexy doctor.'

Sexy? The word seemed to take his breath away.

When was the last time he'd felt...sexy?

Testosterone had had no place in his world for four long years. He couldn't let it. He was still Emma's husband, Jacob's father, son-in-law to Lois and Paul.

But right now the adrenaline from the night's drama was still with him, and it was shifting barriers he'd had no intention of moving. He should turn away, get himself to his end of the house, remember that he was Emma's husband, Jacob's father, Lois and Paul's son-in-law.

But he was something else. Someone else. A someone he'd almost forgotten.

He had to steady himself. He had to remember who he really was, who circumstances had forced him to be.

But right now, conscience, sadness, loss were all fading in the presence of this vibrant, smiling woman. She was looking at him with teasing, questioning eyes.

She was looking at him as if…as if he was a man, she was a woman and the night was theirs to do with as they wanted.

And he did want.

So why not? It was surely just…this night?

They both knew the facts. She'd told him of her past, of her humiliation, and she knew his story as well. The whole world knew his story. Every woman he'd ever met looked at him with sympathy, sadness—even sometimes horror.

But not Jenny, at least…not on this night.

This night…

Her face had changed now. The teasing had gone and there was understanding.

'Rob, four years is a long time,' she said, gently into the night. 'And Rob, I won't intrude. Tell me to back off. It's just…we're both adults. What

I'm feeling now seems pretty right to me, but I won't be hurt or offended—even not too disappointed—if you tell me the feeling's not reciprocated. I'm not expecting commitment here, Dr Pierson. I just thought…fun?'

'Fun?'

'Well, maybe a bit more than fun,' she confessed. 'Maybe warmth and closeness and a bit of human contact we both seem to be missing at the moment.'

'I…' He closed his eyes.

And in that moment something stirred. Anger? Rebellion?

No.

Fun.

The word was suddenly front and centre. *Fun!*

Maybe that was what this night could be about, he thought. To take this lovely woman into his arms, to feel her body, to smile into her laughing eyes…

Fun and so much more.

'You know what?' she managed, and now she sounded almost breathless. 'Your in-laws aren't in my bedroom.'

'Your bedroom?'

'It's the furthest away from Minnie and Jacob,' she said, a trace of insouciance surfacing again.

'Jen…'

'Don't you dare sound shocked,' she said, her eyes flashing with anger again. 'It's just… I've watched how lovely you've been with Anna tonight, how skilled, how gentle, and I've been thinking of how damned sexy you are. And I just thought, suddenly, in between mouthfuls of toast, that if you and I wanted to exorcise some demons together it might be fun. So… If a guy thinks a woman is sexy and interested and free, he might proposition her. No force, just a gentle enquiry. Does it work both ways or have I offended you to the core?'

Sexy and interested and free? As simple as that.

Was he available? Here, in this house echoing with memories, in this night filled with charged emotion, in the silence where Jacob and Minnie lay sleeping and in this world where Emma still lived, but only her body, not her lovely mind…

Here was this woman. Sexy and interested and free.

Jenny spoke again before he could begin to form a response, but now she sounded as if she was struggling to get the words out. He realised that she'd put herself in an impossible position. The words she'd said couldn't be unsaid.

'So back to our separate ends of the house, Dr Pierson?' she managed. 'That's okay. But you know what? I'm not even going to feel vaguely humiliated. I might go back and cuddle Stumpy a bit more until I'm over it, but there's an end. Don't you dare judge me. If you could kindly move to one side, I'm going to bed.'

He should let her. He should simply stand aside and let her pass.

But she didn't move. She was watching him, her eyes wary, her very stance shouting of defiance. And then he thought...*no. It's not defiance. It's courage.*

He knew her well enough now to have seen through the sorry tale of the zigzagged dinner suit and realised the shattering effect it would have had on her. She'd left her job, her friends, her community because she'd needed to get away. He'd have expected her to curl into a ball of self-protection, yet here she was, exposing herself again. To pain?

To judgement? To yet more humiliation?

She was wearing oversized pink pyjamas with blue penguins on them. She was wiry and tough and defiant. She was competent and...and beautiful.

Soul-searingly beautiful.

She was offering fun. For both of them.

'I think,' he said, slowly now, as if every syllable needed to be carefully considered, 'that I might just have reacted all wrong to your...your very interesting idea.'

'Idea?' she queried. 'So not proposition?'

'Idea,' he said, feeling a little more sure of his ground now. 'Or maybe…ideas.' And then he finally allowed himself to voice the idea that had been in his head from almost the moment he'd seen her inside that damned truck, from the moment he'd seen her risking her life to save one old man and his beloved dog. 'Jenny, I think… the moment I saw you I thought… I felt…'

'Desire?' she ventured when he stopped, because he couldn't figure a way to say what he was feeling without it sounding chauvinistic, primeval, inappropriate.

'I guess,' he said helplessly, and then more strongly, 'yes, desire. Jenny, you're so damned beautiful. But I won't hurt you.'

'Eyes wide open,' she said. Her voice was now a husky whisper and he knew without asking that desire was building in her as well as in him. The very air seemed charged with something he didn't understand—or something he'd forgotten existed. 'We both know that if it's good it might lead to something more, but I'm only here until Pete gets back to work.'

'In three months.'

'Less than that now,' she whispered. 'So…so if things get messy we simply go to being formal housemates.'

'If things get messy?'

'Well, if you fall madly, passionately in love with me it might happen,' she said, sounding thoughtful. 'I'm not looking at a long-term relationship here, Dr Pierson, and I imagine neither are you.'

Long-term...

He was over long-term, he thought. Four years of grief, of heartache, of living with the unbearable, and also of facing the massive judgement of his in-laws, had locked something deep inside. That was long-term.

But maybe that long-term lock was disintegrating. This woman in her crazy pyjamas, with her smiling eyes, her voice saying no strings, her words saying she understood...maybe she could help him try.

She was so...

'Jenny,' he managed, and his voice felt so thick he struggled to get the word out.

'I'm here,' she said. And she stretched out her hand and laid it on his arm.

It was enough. That one gesture was enough to break through the grief-stricken barriers of the past four long years. He felt them dissolve, crumple away. He loved Emma, maybe he always would, but with the crumpling of barriers a new truth was suddenly there.

This woman was beautiful and she wanted

him. Simple as that. She was standing before him and what she was offering...

A gift beyond price?

Life.

His hand took hers, locking fingers, feeling the warmth, the firm grip of her decision. His free hand came up to cup her face. His gaze met hers and locked.

'I'm not sure about you,' she whispered. 'But right now I'm over over-thinking. I just need to go to bed. You want to come?'

And how was a man to answer that?

'Jen, are you sure?'

And in answer she stood on her tiptoes. She cupped his face in both her hands and she kissed him. And it was such a kiss... It was deep, warm and sure. It was a kiss of desire, of certainty, an affirmation of something he couldn't even begin to understand.

'I think we're both sure,' she managed when the kiss finally ended, a kiss that had somehow become not her idea, not under her control but somehow something that seemed to have changed something deep within him. So it was no longer Jen kissing and him being kissed, but it was a joining of two passionate people. A man and a woman with mutual desire, mutual need.

Somehow it seemed that things had shattered

inside. The future was suddenly gloriously his. His, with this woman before him.

And he laughed, a deep, rumbly chuckle that seemed to come from deep within, a chuckle he'd forgotten he even had. And with that, he swung her up into his arms, this lovely woman with her crazy pyjamas and her glorious hair and her heart so big, her generous wonderful heart…

'Then that's amazing,' he managed, and he kissed her again, deeply, strongly, and then he whirled her around in his arms so that she put her arms around his neck and clung. 'That's truly, fantastically splendiferous, like a dream come true. So speaking of dreams… You're right. Let's go to bed.'

She woke spooned in his arms, her naked back cradled against his chest, and she felt perfect. This was what bliss felt like, she decided, and then she thought no, bliss wasn't strong enough to describe what she was feeling.

It was as if she'd come home.

The night had been long and languorous and wonderful. At some stage, early on, he'd said, 'Four years, you think I might have forgotten?' but even then, as their bodies had found each other, as skin touched skin, as sensations burned, the thought of skills forgotten were…well, forgotten.

She'd thought the intensity might be too much, that the mating might be fierce and needful for them both, but instead there'd been wonder. A slow exploration of emotion as well as physical need. Touching, tasting, savouring. Lovemaking that had her feeling right now that she was where she was meant to be, where she wanted to be more than anything in the world.

And that thought had to be crazy. This was surely a one-night stand, or at least a temporary pleasure. For heaven's sake, she'd practically seduced him. Maybe she *had* seduced him, using his body as a way to finally rid herself of the humiliation of Darren.

In her mind, in the beginning, that was what she'd told herself what she was doing. Lovemaking as a cure for them both. She knew he was hurting and she hated that he was.

But there was more. She'd seen his skill, his gentleness and his empathy with his small son, with his patients, with Anna—and added to those admittedly very desirable attributes, she'd unashamedly admired the sheer physicality. There'd been desire there, she admitted to herself, and now…rather than that desire being sated…

She wanted to stay where she was for the rest of her life!

But then her phone buzzed into life and she could have cried. They both had their phones by the bedside—of course they did—they were both medical professionals and calls didn't necessarily stop because…well, because both medical professionals were thoroughly sated after a night of pure, unadulterated lust.

Rob woke and sighed as she pulled away, and as she answered the call his hands stayed on her waist. Not breaking the connection.

Please don't let it be a callout, she told herself. Please…

'Jen?'

Frankie.

'Hey,' she said, thinking she should have looked at caller ID before she'd answered. A call from a friend could have been put off.

'You busy?'

'Sort of.'

There was a moment's hesitation. Frankie knew her well.

'You sound half asleep. You're not at work?'

'Um…no. Is this urgent? Can I call you back?'

But maybe Frankie knew her too well. 'You're with someone!' she said in a tone of delight. 'Aren't you?'

'Frankie!'

'Hey, I'm going. But you have to ring and tell me everything. I wanted to talk dog, but it can wait. Eight o'clock in the morning, huh?' She could hear the grin in Frankie's voice. 'There's no urgency, I just had a moment and thought I'd check in. Now I'm very glad I did. You go, girl, right back to what you were doing.'

And the phone went dead.

Yikes. She was now in for an interrogation that'd be no holds barred. She slumped back on the pillows and Rob's arms tightened.

'Sprung,' he said, and she could hear the smile in his voice. He was so close he'd have heard what Frankie had said. 'But…did she say eight?'

'She did.'

The arms were withdrawn a little and he pushed himself up. 'What the…?'

But she was still holding her phone, and on the screen was an unread message. Almost subconsciously, she flicked it through. It was from Minnie.

Jacob and I are heading out for donuts and hot chocolate, and then I'll drop him off at childcare. Stumpy's been out to the lawn and fed. I just popped through to the hospital and everything's peaceful. If I'm right, Rob doesn't have clinic until ten so I'm praying neither of you gets a callout. Enjoy yourselves.

She held it up for Rob to see. He stared at it in bewilderment and then reached for his own phone.

A matching message.

'Did you and Minnie…?' he said slowly as he stared at the screen '…set me up?'

She chuckled at that, because there was no anger in his voice, not even a trace. Instead she heard the beginnings of laughter.

It made her feel…delicious?

'No such thing,' she declared. 'But maybe… well, she did seem to sense that I thought you were sexy.'

'You thought that?' Their phones were tossed aside. He rolled over so he was looking down into her eyes and the desire she could read there was unmistakable. 'You didn't know for sure?'

'Okay, now I'm sure.' She was feeling so good, so lucky. This man was beautiful, and this seemed so right. 'And maybe she did just mention that it's been four long years since your wife died, so maybe it's time…'

And then she paused. His expression had changed. 'What?' she said, bewildered.

'Jen?'

He was still above her, looking down, but the desire had gone. What was in his face now—what? A blankness? Something she had no hope of recognising.

'Mmm?' Something was really wrong. What had she said?

He rolled away and sat up, putting distance, even if only half a pillow's length between them.

'Jen,' he said again, and his voice dragged.

'What?'

'I don't know how… I have no idea. But Jen, Emma isn't dead.'

He told her then, sitting up in bed, a pillow's length apart, the covers pulled up over her breasts because distance suddenly seemed desirable. There'd been a lurch at those first words, the sickening recognition of the feeling she'd had, what, only a couple of months back, when Darren had walked into their hotel room and said, 'My wife is here. You need to leave.'

The sensation was different now, but the emptiness was the same. Only moments ago her world had felt steady and right and wonderful, but now… There was no steadiness here.

'Four years.' Rob's voice was deadpan, expressionless, telling a story that seemed like a recording in his head. 'The haemorrhage caused by the eclampsia was catastrophic, causing irreversible brain damage. Jacob was born at thirty-two weeks and Emma never saw him. For weeks we held onto a desperate hope that there might be something—anything…but nothing. Finally we removed the tracheostomy tube—and then she breathed.'

'By herself?' Her voice was tiny.

'Just for moments.' Still his voice was dead. 'And then…' He closed his eyes. 'Then it ceased, but suddenly Em's mother was screaming at them to put it back in, to help her, to not let it end. And her dad joined in and all I could do was stand back while they made the decision to let their daughter live.'

'You mean…keep their daughter breathing?' There was a difference. She'd been a medical professional for long enough to recognise the scenario. An almost perfect life—perfect apart from one thing. The lack of brain activity. The decision to turn off life support must be soul-searing. 'Oh, Rob…'

'But that was four years ago,' he said, still in that blank, withdrawn voice. 'There's been nothing since, no life, no stimulus response, peg feeding, clear evidence of massive brain damage. But they won't accept it. Lois and Paul are incredibly wealthy, both professional lawyers at the top of their game, and in their grief they can't accept that she's gone. They moved her into a private hospital, they arranged round-the-clock nursing and they've moved heaven and earth to keep her alive. So for almost two years I stayed, caring for Jacob but surrounded by grief and loss and a waiting that could go on for ever.'

She couldn't speak. There seemed nothing she could find to say.

'They wanted Jacob there all the time,' he said, and it was as if repeating a story he knew by heart. '"Jacob's our daughter's baby," Lois kept saying. "If anything can bring her back, the feel of him, the sound of him will do it. She's not dead and her baby needs to be with her." And when I fought it they fought me. Because of that stupid moment when Em signed over medical power of attorney, they applied for her guardianship. I've had to fight to get that reversed—and also fight to reverse the half and half custody arrangement they put in place between me and Emma.'

She stared up, confused and stunned. 'So that's why…' Things were starting to make sense now. Sort of. 'They demanded half and half custody when she's…'

'In this country equal shared custody is normal when parents split,' he told her. 'They simply formalised it when I was too grief-stricken to realise. When I finally surfaced, when I realised Jacob could never have a normal life unless I fought for him, I had to take them to court. I won but they hate me for it.'

He sighed. 'So…the arrangement now is that I take him to Brisbane once a month. That's okay because…well, I still need to see Em myself. I would have built our life there until she…well, I would have liked to be closer. But there's no half measures for Lois and Paul. They take Jacob and sit in that dreadful room and tell him over and over that Mummy loves him, that Mummy will wake one day. But hush, they tell him, and don't touch Mummy, except maybe stroke her hand, but no playing here, nothing. Her room is filled with medical paraphernalia, but it's a place of reverence.'

'But for a baby?' she whispered, horrified, and he grimaced.

'Yeah, not appropriate, or not long-term. By the time he was old enough to register where he was being taken, Jacob was sobbing every time we got near, but if Lois and Paul had control that'd be every day. In the end the only way forward seemed to be to bring him back here. Em and I both loved Willhua, and here he has the chance to be…just a kid.'

Whoa. She felt as if her breath had been sucked right out of her. Their lovemaking had been light and free, but now the ghost of a not-dead wife was suddenly all around them. The idea of a little boy being forced to sit in such a vigil. The thought of Rob with such a load to bear.

The joy of the night had disappeared as if

it had never been, and there seemed no way it could come back. This was too heavy. Too much.

And all at once she thought, *I'm not old enough for this. Not wise enough. I don't have the courage to face this.*

'I thought you knew,' Rob was saying. 'Everyone here knows. I just assumed...'

'People talked about your tragedy,' she whispered. 'I guess... I assumed...death.'

'And it makes a difference,' he said—and it wasn't a question.

But it was a question to Jen. It shouldn't make a difference, she thought. Or should it? Part of her wanted to turn now, take this man in her arms and assure him that it made no difference at all. That the sex and laughter and the pure, free joy of the night could be resumed, just like that.

But this was too big. Too huge.

Maybe it was the shock, the echoes of Darren's betrayal. Maybe it was some sort of inexplicable moral barrier, the thought of Emma lying in a coma while she lay with her husband.

Maybe it was cowardice?

Whatever, all she knew right now was that she needed space. This was doing her head in.

And Rob knew.

'Jen, I'm so sorry,' he told her. 'If I'd guessed...

But even if you'd gone into it knowing, I should never have...'

'You think it's wrong?' she whispered, watching his face. 'There's part of you that thinks being with me is...a betrayal?'

'No. I...' He paused and shook his head, as if struggling to find words. 'Jen, I don't know what to think. I loved Em. I still do. When I see her now there's grief, but it's like visiting a shrine. The difference is that instead of a monument there's a living, breathing woman.'

'I can see that.' She put her hand on his face and said gently, 'Rob, I'm sorry. I'm so, so sorry.' But her feelings were threatening to overwhelm her. She was close to tears, but the last thing Rob needed was weeping. She had to get away. 'Rob... I... I need to take a shower. I need...'

'To back off? Of course you do.'

And there was nothing she could say to deny it. There was just...nothing.

'I'm so sorry,' she whispered again. 'But I need to go.'

CHAPTER EIGHT

SHE FELT SHATTERED.

There was a part of her, the cowardly part, that wanted to do exactly what she'd done after Darren's betrayal. Pull up stumps and leave this whole complicated mess. Deal with the confusion in her heart by running. To do so, though, would be hurtful, a declaration that somehow she'd been betrayed.

And she hadn't. She stood under the shower and forced her mind to replay every conversation she'd ever had with anyone about this man, everything he'd ever said to her.

About the tragedy that was Emma.

Those first days on the job had been frantic. The first time she'd worked alongside Gary had been the night of the truck accident. It had been intense, tragic, lurching her from knowing little about her working partners to being involved up to her ears.

Gary had spoken to her briefly about Rob, but

in those first meetings there'd been no opportunity to delve into Rob's personal life. To do so then would have seemed…creepy? Certainly less than respectful.

If she'd started work on the Monday to normal activity, if things had been less frenetic, Gary would probably have given her the lowdown on the town and its inhabitants. He surely would have told her then about Rob's background. But that first night had catapulted her from being an outsider to being Rob's housemate. From that night on, Gary would simply have assumed she knew.

And Rob? Same thing. This was a small town. Everyone knew everyone's business. He'd spoken briefly about the tragedy. She'd wondered why his in-laws had such ongoing influence, she'd been astounded that he'd worry they could apply for custody, but he'd never lied. He'd just assumed…

Stupid, stupid, stupid, she told herself. To assume that here was a gorgeous, sexy man with a perfect little son who was…

Ripe for the taking?

She'd practically seduced him.

She felt herself cringing as she stood under the steaming water. Her actions the night before now seemed totally inappropriate.

Why? Because Emma wasn't dead.

Because Rob was still legally married.

Maybe this was Darren's legacy, she told herself. Maybe the humiliation of finding out about her boss's wife was still with her.

Or maybe she was imagining Emma.

The walls seemed to be closing in on her. She was being stupid, she told herself. No one had lied to her. She'd thought Emma was dead, but wasn't she? Brain death was surely death, even if the body kept functioning. There was no need for shame or humiliation, or even regret.

But she did feel these things.

Finally she dried and dressed and headed for the laundry. Stumpy was fast asleep—she was healing nicely but she was quite happy to be woken and hugged.

'Dogs are safer,' she whispered into her over-large ears. 'Dogs are far less complicated. If your bed here was a little bit bigger I might even be tempted to join you.'

And Rob?

He headed back to his end of the house and did exactly the same thing. He hit the shower.

He felt ill.

Last night had been almost miraculous. A magic sliver of rainbow in a life that for the last few years had seemed an unbroken grey. Jenny's smile, her laughter, her body, her unadulterated joy in their joining—for a while during the night he'd thought this could be what life might be like. There could be a future without this overwhelming sense of loss and betrayal.

Because betrayal was all around him now. Emma was still a warm, living being, his wife, the mother of his son. He hadn't made it clear to Jenny that she was still alive. He'd just assumed.

How could he possibly have assumed something so important? He had no right. He'd seen the shock on Jenny's face and he'd thought... *she's feeling betrayed.*

Had he betrayed Em? Had he betrayed both women?

When could he let go? Never.

Last night, as he'd held Jenny in his arms, the years of bleakness had faded. He'd...loved.

Loved? It was a strong word, surely too strong after only two short weeks, but she was gorgeous, clever, strong, funny—a way forward?

A way out of this grey fog he lived in?

Was it no accident that Jenny hadn't realised Em was still alive? Taking her to bed, loving her, had that been a lie on his part? A betrayal to both women?

This was doing his head in. He needed to get out of the shower and go talk to her. Damn that he and Jacob were due to fly to Brisbane tonight. It was the worst possible timing.

Or maybe it was the best. It'd give them both time and space to come to terms with…

With reality. That he was still married. That he couldn't move on, that he was trapped in a life he couldn't begin to understand.

So much for rainbows, he told himself as he dried and dressed and readied himself for the day.

Rainbows were fleeting, an ephemeral illusion.

So was the idea of loving Jenny.

They met over breakfast. Jen was wearing her paramedic uniform. She looked clean, fit— lovely. She was sitting at the table spreading marmalade on her toast when he entered.

'Good morning. There's coffee in the pot.' As a first approach into a morning-after conversation it wasn't exactly helpful, but it was something.

'Jen, I'm so sorry.'

'There's nothing to be sorry for,' she said. 'Or maybe there is. I'm sorry for you, sorry for Jacob, sorry for this whole situation, but you don't need to apologise to me.' And then she looked up from her toast and attempted a smile. 'I had a very nice time, thank you, Dr Pierson. You make a great lay.'

He hadn't known what to expect, but it wasn't

this. The teasing laughter was back in her eyes. Maybe it was a shield, he thought, but if so it was a very good shield. And it was a shield she was asking him to share.

'Thank you,' he managed, mock modest, and she chuckled. And then she looked ruefully down into the jar she was holding. 'I appear to have finished your marmalade. Sorry, Dr Pierson, but you're on Vegemite. I should have saved you some but…' she sighed, mock theatrically '…but I didn't. So now you know. I'm not good at sharing. Bed for one night is great, but any more than that… Not a good idea.'

And she met his gaze and held. There was a long silence while all sorts of things were unsaid but present for all that.

'Not?' he said at last.

'Not,' she repeated, and was it his imagination or did her voice tremble a little? And then she shrugged and her voice became serious. 'Rob, this isn't a situation I can face. I don't have the courage. A one-night fling might be great—it was great—but let's leave it there.'

He nodded. Courage… It'd take more than that to move into a relationship with him, he thought.

A relationship?

He was married. Emma still lived. What had he been thinking?

'But don't you dare feel bad about it,' she said,

the bounce returning to her voice. She stood up, toast in hand. 'You know, I'm betting your Emma wouldn't begrudge you last night one bit. I wouldn't if I was her. So no guilt, from either of us. You're going to Brisbane tonight?'

'I...yes. We drive to Sydney and then fly.'

'It's a pain of a trip.'

'We're used to it. Angus is on call while I'm away. Have you met him yet? He's great—he was the family doctor here for thirty years. He's in his seventies, but trying to retire to potter in his veggie garden. He took over again during... in the years after Jacob was born and he looks after things now when I need to be away.' He was talking too fast, he thought. Trying to drive away the emotions of the morning.

The feeling of shame?

Shame. Was that what this was? Shame for loving this woman last night. Shame for enjoying her body when Emma was still...

'Don't!' What was it about her that made her guess what he was feeling? She put down her toast and stepped forward so she was standing right in front of him, hands on hips. 'Don't you dare analyse last night, make it something it wasn't. It was two adults having fun, nothing more and nothing less. So put it behind you and go to Brisbane.'

'How did you know...?'

'Let's call it a good guess,' she told him and then she put her hands on his shoulders, raised herself on her toes and kissed him on the mouth, but very lightly, a feather touch, no more.

'You're a very nice man, Dr Pierson,' she said as the kiss ended. 'And, as I said, you're a very good lay. It was a lovely night, but that's all it was. Now, I'm thinking you need to eat your breakfast and go see some patients. I hope Anna and her little one are okay this morning. Meanwhile, Gary and I are scheduled to bring Moira Gardner home from Whale Head. Apparently her hip operation was a resounding success—you know she's booked in here for a couple of days' aftercare? You'll still be here this afternoon to admit her? Great. So we're both busy and it's time for us to move on.'

And then she gave a fierce little nod, as if she was cementing something into her mind.

Then she picked up her toast and departed.

CHAPTER NINE

WORK WAS HER SALVATION, and she was lucky because Friday was busy.

By the time she returned to the house that night Rob and Jacob had left. 'They'll be back Monday morning,' Minnie told her when she walked in. It was almost six o'clock. Minnie was taking a lasagne to the oven, and the smell made her feel like she…well, like she was home. But this wasn't her home. This weekend was time out from a situation she didn't know how to deal with.

'You shouldn't be here,' she told Minnie. 'I can look after myself.'

'I thought you might be up for a home-cooked meal,' the older woman told her. 'By the look on Rob's face as he left…well, he always looks strained when he leaves, but this afternoon it was another level. I'm hoping you're not feeling the same.'

'A bit,' she admitted and then thought…why

not say it like it was? Minnie had practically played the part of matchmaker here. It was surely appropriate to be honest. 'I hadn't realised Emma was still alive,' she said, and she knew she couldn't keep pain and shock from her voice.

'Oh, my dear.' The woman's face crumpled and she put the lasagne down on the table as if it was suddenly far too heavy. 'Oh, my dear! Oh, for heaven's sake, how…?'

'I have no idea. But it…makes a difference.'

'It does.' Minnie sat, suddenly looking every day of her seventy-odd years. 'I thought…we all assumed… I mean, the whole town knows the story.'

'Yeah,' she said bitterly, and headed for the fridge. 'Wine?'

'Yes,' Minnie said definitely. 'My dear, does it make a difference?'

'You must see that it does.'

'I can't imagine he concealed it deliberately,' she ventured. 'If that's any help. It's no secret.'

'No. He told no lies. It's just…' She shook her head. 'It makes things way too complicated in my head.'

'And those in-laws of his make things so much worse,' Minnie ventured. 'They can't get away from their grief and they expect Rob to stay in the same state of perpetual mourning. Speaking of in-laws…'

'Are we speaking of in-laws?'

'Well, parents,' Minnie said and smiled, a sort of sideways smile that said this was an obvious attempt to change the subject. 'You should see Anna's parents.'

'The Windsors? They're not giving Anna a hard time, are they?'

'The opposite.' Minnie relaxed. 'Rob had them in his clinic this morning and talked to them for ages. And when they came out Marjorie went straight to the baby shop. I hear she practically bought the place out of everything blue, and Graham drove to Whale Head to buy a cot and a pram because nothing here was good enough. And they're telling the world that their grandson has arrived, as if they've been counting the days for the last eight months, and Marjorie already has a phone full of baby pictures. Things could have gone the opposite way, but now... thanks to Rob...and to you...they've decided to go with pride.'

'Well, good for them,' she managed, and she knew, she just knew, that Rob would have told them of his own background. Despite her confusion, the muddle in her own heart, she found herself smiling. Feeling...pride? Pride in Rob?

She had no right to feel pride, she told herself. He was nothing to do with her. A colleague. A landlord. A one-night stand?

'So what will you do now?' Minnie asked tentatively and she thought…what?

'I'll go and see Anna.'

'That's lovely. Rob said to tell you she's been asking for you. But after that?'

'I have no idea.' She sighed and sat down. 'Lasagne first. Anna second. And then…maybe a weekend on my own to figure where to take things from here?'

And then the weekend seemed to take on a life of its own. Angus took over in the hospital. She met him on Saturday morning and instantly liked him, an elderly doctor who looked more like a gardener than a medic.

'I keep my registration current, just to give Rob a break,' he told her when she met him finishing a ward round. 'But I miss my garden. Just lucky the ground's waterlogged after all this rain, or I'd be suffering withdrawal.'

She and Gary were at the hospital to collect Olivia Hoffman and take her home. Olivia had had a fall a couple of days back. The ninety-six-year-old had been waiting until her daughter could clear her schedule to come and stay with her, but her seventy-five-year-old daughter wasn't confident about driving her mum along the winding cliff road to her farm.

'They look about as old as each other,' Jen

commented as Gary finished tucking both women into the ambulance.

'It's this place,' Angus said. 'You don't age, you just sort of pickle. The salt wind does that to you, like herrings.' He motioned to Olivia's daughter. 'Hildy's on the hospital board, she's a volunteer at the charity shop and she takes part-time care of her three grandchildren. Olivia's only just retired from the charity shop as well. That's what I intend to look like at ninety-six too,' he told her. 'This is such a great place to grow old. So you've been here for two weeks. Ready to put down roots yet?'

With that he met her gaze, his look kindly but a little quizzical. And Jen wondered just how much talk there was already about a young female paramedic moving into the doctor's house.

'It's far too soon to tell,' she said, a bit too brusquely, and he nodded, his look a bit too understanding for her liking.

'It takes courage to move into a whole new situation,' he said gently. 'But they tell me you abseiled down a cliff to try and save Charlie Emerson. A woman like that…she'd have courage for anything.'

'Not anything.'

'Maybe not.' He hesitated. 'It's women,' he said slowly, as if he was thinking it through. 'I've just been talking to Anna in there, holding her baby but declaring she'll sit her exams because she's darned if she'll waste all of the study she's been doing this year. And when her dad said, "Why not wait a year, let things settle?" Marjorie flashed at him, "Let what settle? Everything's settled already." Women,' he said again. 'Courage in spades. And you…abseiling, taking on the role of Willhua paramedic…' His voice softened still further. 'And maybe you and Rob?'

'Has Minnie been talking to you?' she demanded, hands on hips.

'Maybe,' he said. 'Minnie and I go back a long way, and Minnie's feeling bad.'

'She shouldn't feel bad.'

'She's worried that you'll leave.'

She sighed, thinking that'd be the easy option. But she'd signed up for the three-month stint. To leave now…

'I'll stay working,' she told Angus. 'But…'

'But the rest is none of my business?'

'I wish it wasn't *my* business,' she told him and then she thought of Rob and Emma, and the situation with Jacob and his in-laws, and the whole tragic mess. 'From now on… I can't see how it can be.'

The call on Sunday morning was to Ruth Corben, a sixty-year-old woman who bred alpacas on a small farm a couple of kilometres inland.

On her distressed call she'd said she'd suffered a fall and had struggled to reach her phone. She was still on the floor.

'She's been suffering from myelofibrosis,' Gary told Jen on the way there. 'She was diagnosed about four years ago. It's a bugger.'

Jen knew the condition, a rare form of chronic leukaemia that caused disruption of normal production of blood cells. Left unchecked it could cause severe anaemia, with associated weakness and fatigue. It could simmer for years, but flare-ups had to be treated fast to avoid the leukaemia transforming to acute.

The thought of Ruth lying alone on the farmhouse floor, was enough for speed, lights and sirens, and when they got there they both wished they could have got there faster. Ruth was crumpled on the kitchen floor, weeping with pain and with frustration. By the look of her face, she'd been weeping for a while.

'I tripped on the back step,' she told them. 'And I couldn't get up. It took me so long to crawl back in here and get the phone off the table.'

'Which is why Rob asked you to wear the alarm,' Gary scolded, his tone not hiding his anxiety. He was feeling her pulse while Jen did a fast visual examination. 'What hurts?'

'Everything hurts. And I don't need it! Stupid thing.'

'You do need it, Ruth! What hurts?'

'Nothing. Everything. My ankle. I must have twisted it when I fell. But I haven't even fed the animals yet. I have ten alpacas,' she said, looking helplessly up at Jen. 'And Betty's pregnant and Bosun needs me.'

They'd already met Bosun, a gorgeous young border collie who'd raced out to meet them and then raced back to his mistress. Now he was lying flat on the floor a few feet back, crouched as if in readiness to…save his mistress? But he seemed to be almost quivering in anxiety. Did he know they were there to help?

'I'll just need another iron transfusion,' Ruth managed. 'Could you ring Rob? He'll tell you. If you could just help me feed everyone, then you could take me down to the hospital and I'll be home by dinner. Betty's almost due to give birth. I have to stay.'

'Angus's on call this weekend,' Gary told her. 'And I know what he'll say.' He gave Jen a fleeting glance that was information all by itself. He'd been feeling her pulse, listening to her heart, and they'd both seen the greyish tinge to her face that said this wasn't all about a fall. 'There's no way he'll let you come home to be alone tonight. Is there anyone you can call?'

'My daughter's overseas,' she whispered, more distressed. 'I told her to go, don't worry about me. She and her husband have been saving for years. They're in Venice and I won't let you worry her. Please…ring Rob. He knows how important it is for me to stay home.'

There was a moment's silence while Gary considered. Jen stayed in the background, organising injections for pain. Gary knew this woman, he knew the situation.

'Give Rob a call,' Gary told Jen at last. 'On speaker. Ruth, will you do what he says?' He nodded to Jen. 'Rob won't mind you ringing—he'd want us to contact him. Angus will concur. Rob's been there for Ruth…'

'Since I got this damned thing,' Ruth whispered. 'He knows how important it is that my daughter has a holiday. I have to stay here.'

So while Gary worked on, Jen rang Rob. He answered almost on the first ring. 'Jen?'

And what was there in that to make her heart clench? The way he said her name. As if he needed it to be her?

Where was he? By Emma's side? With his in-laws? This was doing her head in.

'Rob, Gary and I are with Ruth Corben,' she told him, trying to make her voice practical, professional. 'You're on speaker so we're all listening. Ruth's had a fall. The only obvious damage we can see this early is her ankle, which we hope is just twisted, but she didn't have the strength to get herself up. It seems to have taken her over an hour to get to the phone. What she wants is a quick trip to hospital, an iron infusion and to be brought home again tonight. She's listening now. Would you have time to talk to her or should we ring back when we have her down in Willhua?'

'I'm not going anywhere until I've talked to Rob,' Ruth said, starting to weep again. The long wait on the floor must have frightened her to the stage where she was acting purely on instinct. 'Rob, please tell them. I can't go. All I need is some iron.'

'Could you wait just a moment?' Rob said quietly. 'I need to step outside where it's quiet. Jen, can you put the phone near Ruth?'

What followed was a wait, interrupted by a muted, muffled announcement…

'Could the owner of a Mercedes parked in the ambulance bay please report to Reception immediately?'

He must be in hospital, Jen thought, recognising the sound of an intercom. Emma's hospital? She closed her eyes, and when she opened them Gary was watching her. With sympathy?

Already? Had word got around so fast? Or was it clearly obvious how she was feeling towards this man?

But when Rob came back on the line he was professional, kind, firm, definite. The phone was still on speaker but he was speaking only to Ruth.

'Ruth, you had an iron infusion two weeks ago,' he told her. 'And the one before that was recent too. You know we talked this through, and we talked to Ben, your oncologist in Sydney. He said then that you'll need a blood transfusion and tests to see if another round of chemotherapy is called for. I'd like to ring him now to tell him to expect you.'

'But I can't go to Sydney,' Ruth stammered. 'You know I can't.'

'And you know the alternative,' Rob said, his voice becoming even more gentle. 'Come on, Ruth. Lorraine and Peter are overseas right now having a babymoon. Your first grandchild's due in three months. You want to miss that?'

'No, I...'

'Of course you don't. Ruth, your grandbaby needs you. Your alpacas need you and so does Bosun. So you want to live, but you need to accept what's necessary to make that happen.'

'If you tell me what to do, I can feed the alpacas before we go,' Jen offered. 'At least, I think I can. Is it complicated?'

'Just...hay.'

'Well, I can heave hay bales with the best of

them. You said Betty's pregnant. Is Betty an alpaca?'

'Yes, I need to check her. And Bosun...'

'I'm already looking after one dog,' Jen told her. 'Why not two? And I'm trained in home births. How different can an alpaca be? I don't mind coming up here to check and feed them until someone else can take over. If your doctor says you don't need chemo you might be home in a couple of days.'

There was silence from all of them. Gary was looking at her, his brows raised. Ruth was staring at her as if she was...her best hope? And Rob... Who knew what he was thinking, but it was Rob who broke the silence first.

'There you go, Ruth. Problem sorted for today. Gary and Jen will take you down to Willhua, Angus will make sure you're stable and we'll organise a transfer to Sydney. I'll be back tomorrow. I'll ring you and Ben, and we'll sort something permanent then.'

'Permanent?' Ruth whispered.

'Until you're strong again,' Rob told her. 'If you accept our advice and help, I know you will be.'

He disconnected and headed back to Emma's ward. Emma's shrine. That was how it felt, how it had felt for years. He walked in and Lois had put Jacob back on Emma's bed, forcing his hand to stroke his mother's. Or what had been his mother. The pallid, lifeless figure under the perfect bedding seemed almost a ghost of what had been his Emma.

Jacob had that stoic look. He was used to this, a ritual where his grandparents insisted he sit on his mother's bed, but he hated it. What four-year-old would sit reverently beside someone... who wasn't there?

There was a basket of building blocks and random toys in the corner. Whenever Rob was in the room he was allowed to play with them, but Lois wanted a connection between Jacob and his mother.

But the slight, still figure in the bed had no connection left to give. Rob's heart clenched, as it did every time he saw her. His beautiful Emma.

How dare they leave her like this?

But anger didn't help, and he fought it down as he'd done for years. It wasn't their fault they couldn't get past their grief, and anger didn't help. But Jacob was looking up at him and wriggling forcefully, until finally he was permitted to get down.

'I want to home,' he said fiercely to his father. 'Daddy, can we go home?'

'Home should be here,' Lois said almost as

fiercely, and Rob's anger was tempered, as it always was, by the knowledge that Lois was struggling, as she always did, to hold back tears. Lois was here alone this weekend—it seemed Paul was away on business. 'He'll be back on Monday,' Lois had told them, unable to keep bitterness from her voice. 'Unlike you, he'll never stay away from our Emma for long. Rob, please make Jacob sit back on the bed.'

'We're going for an ice cream,' Rob told her as Jacob's chin wobbled toward mutiny. 'We'll be back in half an hour.'

'You know the court says we control what happens on our access weekend.'

She was right. Legally, it was Emma who had control, and her unbreakable power of attorney meant that Lois and Paul were her voice. The more Rob fought it, the more obsessive they became.

Grief did appalling things to people. He knew it and he tried his best to make allowances, but this was impossible. So far, all his legal challenges had achieved was the agreement that when Jacob was with his mother, Rob would be there too.

Right now he could insist Jacob leave with him but he'd learned there were easier ways.

'We both know that's true, Lois,' he said gently. 'But I'm about to buy an ice cream and eat it downstairs. Are you saying you want me to leave Jacob here with you and have my ice cream by myself?'

Lois looked at Jacob and had the sense to know that Rob walking out would lead to a full-scale meltdown.

'Half an hour,' she whispered.

'You could join us.'

'Not when I can stay here. Someone has to.'

CHAPTER TEN

AN HOUR LATER Jen walked through into the back yard of the doctor's residence, and unclipped Bosun's lead. To alleviate Ruth's distress they'd brought the collie back with them in the ambulance. Ruth had hugged him all the way, but now Angus had her in his care.

Ruth's ankle was being X-rayed and stabilised, and the chopper from South Sydney Air Rescue was due to pick her up in an hour. Gary and Jen would be needed then to take her the short distance to the football field where the chopper would land, but until then Jen had time to settle. And introduce Bosun to Stumpy.

This was some imposition, she thought. One dog became two in the house. But Rob had heard her make the offer on the phone and hadn't objected.

There'd be so much going on in his life that one more dog could hardly make a difference, she thought, and Bosun was gorgeous. Beautifully trained, quiet, subdued—well, of course he would be—he still reacted to a rub behind the ears with a cautious tail wag. And when Stumpy limped out of the laundry to meet him, the two dogs did mutual nose and tail sniffing and then started a slow perambulation of the yard.

It was almost as if Stumpy was showing Bosun around, Jen thought, and smiled to see them. The continued effort to find any of Charlie's friends or family who'd want her had proved fruitless, but after two weeks Jen was starting to hope they'd never find anyone. Stumpy was still subdued, but she was warm and cuddly, and more and more Jen was treating her as a trusted confidante.

'Look after each other, you guys,' she told them, and headed inside. She needed lunch before she was needed for the chopper transfer. She walked through to the kitchen—and stopped dead. A stranger was sitting at the kitchen table.

The man was immaculately groomed, in what she recognised as the casual clothes of the upper classes—crisp chinos, brand name loafers, a classy shirt with a discreet woven logo and a bomber jacket she'd seen in advertisements that fleetingly appeared on her social media forays—but only fleetingly because social media algorithms seemed somehow to recognise paramedics' salaries.

And the man himself? He was in his sixties, with silver fox hair, tanned complexion and blue eyes that seemed...cautious.

He was cautious? This man was sitting at *her* kitchen table, she told herself. She needed to remind herself of that, because she'd realised who he must be.

She paid rent. This man didn't, but he still had a place in this house. In the formal living room there was photo after photo of a baby, a small girl, a teenager growing to womanhood. Emma with her two parents, and one of them was this man.

This was Emma's father.

'Mr...' She stopped. She didn't know his surname, she realised.

She didn't know anything. She was so out of her depth.

'I've been waiting for two hours,' he said, his tone letting her know he was displeased.

Keep it light, she told herself. What use was conflict, and this man had lost...was losing?... his daughter.

'Were you waiting for me? I had no idea. Sorry, but I've been working,' she told him, making a slight gesture to her uniform. It helped, she decided, having it on. It made her feel professional, as if this guy could be just a problem patient.

'Ah, yes,' he said, still sounding irritated. 'Tony tells me you work for the ambulance service.'

'Tony?' She thought of the guy watching them in the playground. 'The guy in the car?'

'Tony Lester. He's a security agent. We pay him to keep an eye on our grandson, on our daughter's behalf.'

'Really?' She was having trouble here, but the last thing needed was escalation to anger. 'I can't imagine why that's necessary—Rob seems such a good dad, but I guess that's not my business. I'm only a tenant. Would you like a cup of tea? Lunch?'

'No, thank you.'

'But you wanted to see me?'

'Tony told me about you.'

'Really?' She hesitated and then forged on. 'Sorry, but I need to eat,' she said, and headed for the refrigerator. 'I'm on a fast break from work.'

There was method in what she was doing. If she made herself a sandwich while she talked it'd give her something to do with her hands. Also she could turn her back on him, giving her space to catch her breath. 'So what…what can I do for you?'

'Lois and I have decided you need to be spoken to without Rob's interference.'

Whoa. There was so much in that sentence

that she felt winded. She didn't turn from the fridge, though, just found the sliced bread, retrieved two slices and started buttering. What would she put in her sandwich? Who cared?

'Could you look at me, please?' he said.

'I'm on my lunch break. I have a patient transfer in thirty minutes. I need to eat and run.'

'What I have to say is important.'

'So's my patient's life. Her transfer is urgent.'

'Is her life more important than my daughter's?'

That brought her around. She swivelled and stared blankly at him. 'What…what on earth do you mean?'

'My daughter's marriage is important to her.' And his voice suddenly cracked—with grief? With anger? She could hardly differentiate. 'What's happening now…if she found out about you…it could kill her.'

'Do I have it wrong?' she whispered. 'Emma's been in an unresponsive coma for four years. No?'

And his face twisted, grief and anger combined. 'You don't have permission to use her name!'

Whoa.

But, strangely, this helped, for suddenly Jen found herself slipping into medical mode.

For four years this man and his wife had kept

watch over a beloved daughter, had refused to let her go. What was happening now…he sounded on the edge of sanity.

And with that realisation, professional training kicked in. There was no use escalating a conflict here. There was no use trying to reason. She had to do whatever was needed to de-escalate.

'No,' she said, meeting his gaze head-on. 'I don't have your permission. I apologise.'

'I need you to do more than that. I need you to leave.'

'That's tricky,' she said, still quietly. 'I'm not sure what Tony told you, but I rent a room here from the hospital board. This is a hospital house, for hospital medics.'

'It's my daughter's house.'

She nodded, still carefully calm. 'I can understand that's how it must feel.'

'And you have no place here. Not with my grandson, and not with *him*.' And he said *him* with such a mix of emotion that she physically flinched.

But it still wasn't her place to escalate anger. This wasn't about her. It was Rob who had to face this situation over and over. He'd have to negotiate this anger…for the rest of his life?

This situation was beyond her and suddenly she knew it. She'd known Rob for what, two weeks? The shock of finding Emma was alive was still with her and, logical or not, it had piled on the humiliation of Darren's betrayal. There could be no comparison, yet her bruised heart was struggling to come to terms with both.

She was the 'other woman'. Darren had done that to her—he'd treated her as his lover and all the time there'd been a wife, a true love, in the background.

This was so different and yet...maybe it wasn't? She was still the outsider in this mess.

'Rob and I are friends,' she said slowly. 'And so are Jacob and I. I'm here as a housemate.'

'You shared a bedroom on Thursday night.'

And that seemed to suck all the air from her lungs. 'What the...?' She couldn't find words.

'His bedroom lights didn't go on at all,' he snapped. 'Yours stayed on until after midnight and there were two people. There were two shadows behind the drapes.'

'Did Tony tell you that?' She could hardly get the words out.

'Of course he did.'

'I can't believe...'

But she couldn't make herself go on. She didn't have the words.

This man's actions were beyond reason, and she should respond with fury. Half of her did, but overriding her anger was another emotion. She just felt...smirched.

She was the 'other woman', caught up in a sordid domestic triangle that was none of her doing. She hadn't known. Rob hadn't betrayed her deliberately as Darren had but, logical or not, that was how she felt now. Betrayed.

Lost.

Somehow she had to keep calm. She put her fingers up and touched the paramedic insignia on her uniform, a gesture she used professionally when dealing with drunks or addicts throwing invective at her. Situations all paramedics had to deal with.

Her insignia reminded her to take a deep breath and stay professional. That was what she needed to do now—treat this guy as if he was ill—as maybe he was.

But, unlike an injured drunk, she had no obligation to stay, no obligation to treat. So wind this up and get out of here.

'Your…your relationship with your son-in-law and your grandson might be your business,' she managed. 'But my life is my own. Spying on my bedroom is not right. It might even be illegal. So I'm sorry you've come all this way to see me, but this conversation is done.'

Enough. She turned back to the counter, grabbed a jar of Vegemite and smeared a thick black layer on the bottom slice of bread. Then she slapped the top layer on and bit deliberately into her sandwich.

The Vegemite was so thick it almost made her gag, but she was fighting for dignity here. She didn't gag. She even managed to swallow as she headed for the door.

But what she saw there… The man's face had crumpled and he looked close to tears. 'Please,' he said, and he almost sounded…broken. 'This is my daughter's house. Please just leave.'

She didn't go straight back to work. There was time before the transfer. Instead she went out into the back yard and shared her sandwich with Bosun and Stumpy.

Or tried to share. It seemed they weren't all that keen on inch-thick Vegemite either. It had started raining and they came to sit with her on the veranda, but the sandwich stayed uneaten.

My life is my own.

Those words had come from her mouth almost as a resolution, something deep within telling her what she must do. She hugged the dogs and thought of the difficulties of going back to Lorna's—with two dogs now. Impossible. Or leaving town. That was hardly fair. The town needed her and she'd committed to three months.

Besides, she'd be running away. She thought

of the wonder of being with Rob, of the way she'd felt in his arms, of the pure joy.

She didn't deserve such joy. He was Emma's. She was indeed 'the other woman'.

Dear heaven, that was twisted. That was channelling Paul and his grief-twisted opinions. If her logic held true…if she didn't deserve joy, then neither must Rob. For ever and for ever and for ever?

'I don't know what to do,' she whispered to the dogs and then her phone pinged and it was Angus. 'Ruth would like to talk to you before the chopper comes,' he told her. 'Could you come?'

Work. Her salvation. Hooray.

'I'm on my way,' she told him and hugged the dogs goodbye and headed across to the hospital. But as she went she knew Paul was still sitting in the kitchen. Waiting for what?

'I'm on my way,' she said again, but a part of her was thinking…

On her way to where?

Angus was waiting for her, looking worried. His face cleared when he saw her. 'I was about to come and find you,' he told her. 'I saw the Corvette outside the house. Paul and Lois always hire the same car when they fly down from Brisbane. Are they both there?'

'Just Paul,' she said briefly, and the elderly

doctor looked closely at her and then reached out and gripped her shoulder.

'I'm sorry. You know they're…not stable.'

'I know it now.'

'I should have spelt it out more clearly. You've met Chris, our local cop. Would you like me to give him a call? If Paul went into the house without Rob there… Well, there have been instances before. They tried to redecorate Jacob's room a few months back and Rob finally got so angry he had them evicted. I think…well, I know that Emma's condition has left them almost crazy. They can't let her go—they can't let anything go.'

She winced, thinking of that formal sitting room, thinking of what they'd like to do to a little boy's room. Compared to that, what had just happened seemed minor. 'I can handle it,' she said. 'But Ruth?'

He gave her a searching look but moved on. 'She's frantic,' he admitted. 'Rob rang the oncologist in Sydney and they've talked it through. I gather Ruth was advised to start chemo six months ago and the oncologist says she must start now. But that means a six-week stay in Sydney. Her sister lives near South Sydney Hospital, so accommodation's no problem, but she's frantic about Bosun and her alpacas. Her daughter and son-in-law moved in the last time she had chemo, but she won't hear of asking them to come home now. But I gather you offered to keep an eye on them. Could you reassure her?'

'Of course I will.'

'Thank you.' But his grip on her shoulder tightened again. A gesture of comfort and support. 'Paul's upset you.'

'I can handle it,' she said, trying to sound light. 'This situation's horrid, but really, it's nothing to do with me.'

'Isn't it?' The elderly man's eyes were kind and watchful and she thought that a lifetime of being a family doctor would have given him insights now that were far from welcome. So why not be honest?

'I guess maybe,' she whispered. 'If it really isn't…why does that make me feel…desolate?'

The chopper landed on the football oval twenty minutes later, just as the first clap of thunder and a sweep of hailstones heralded a storm front. Which meant delay. To Jen's delight, though, Frankie was on board. The crew elected to stay with the chopper, but Jen wasn't going to miss a chance to catch up. She drove her own car out to the football field where the chopper had landed.

'We have time for coffee,' Frankie decreed, after they'd hugged under mutual umbrellas and dived for the cover of the car. 'This is happening all the time at the moment. There's flooding inland and we've been busy with patients trapped by cut roads. They're saying it'll get worse before it gets better though, and right now…this is great. Your place is part of the hospital, right? Can we head there for coffee?'

And Jen thought of Paul. What was he doing? Still sitting at the kitchen table? Or standing in that appalling living room, feeding his grief?

'No,' she said, a bit too brusquely, and Frankie looked quickly at her face—and then nodded.

'Café it is, then,' she agreed, and then she said nothing until they were settled at the back of Willhua's only coffee shop, with a couple of mugs of pretty ordinary coffee in front of them.

'Ugh!' Frankie said as she tasted it. 'I hope you don't normally drink this stuff.'

'Rob has a great coffeemaker.' But for the life of her she couldn't keep the strain out of her voice.

'So… Rob?' Her friend sat back in her chair and eyed her with care. 'Rob was the guy with you when I phoned?'

'I…yes.'

'And you sounded lit up like a Christmas tree.'

'Maybe.'

'But now…not so much?'

And Jen met her friend's gaze and knew there was no point in lying.

'I've just found out he's married,' she said

bluntly. And then she told her, the whole sad situation, ending up with Paul's close to madness demand, the impossibility of going forward... and how unutterably confused she felt.

'Oh, Jen, I'm so sorry,' Frankie said at last. 'But you really like this guy, right?'

'I...yes. But...'

'But what?'

'But it's just too sad,' she said. Then she tilted her chin, and metaphorically squared her shoulders. 'And complicated. But I've only known him for two weeks and I have no right to feel... how I'm feeling. So I think I have a plan. I'm moving out of the house this afternoon.'

'You're *what*?'

'The lady you're about to take to Sydney has given me a solution.'

And she told Frankie about Ruth.

Her conversation with Ruth had been brief and emotional, and in the end it had handed her a way out. Ruth had sounded close to desperation at the thought of leaving her animals alone, and with Paul's vindictiveness still in her head the solution had seemed obvious.

'Ruth's farm's just out of town,' she told her friend. 'She has alpacas and a border collie named Bosun, and she'll need to be in Sydney for maybe six weeks. I offered to move in and take care of them all and she fell on my offer like it was manna from heaven. I now have a place to live. So moving on…'

'Wow,' Frankie said softly and then, thoughtfully, 'So…you're running away again?'

'I am not running. I'm just…'

'Jen, you loved your job with us,' Frankie said, cutting her off. 'And yet you left. And now…do you love living with this guy?'

She flushed. Did she?

'It's only been two weeks,' she muttered. 'It's far too soon to know. And I'm not running far.'

'But still running.'

'Leave it, Frankie,' she said, more angrily than she meant to. What was Frankie suggesting? That there was an element of cowardice in what she was doing?

Well, maybe Frankie was right, she conceded, but how to be brave enough to face the situation in that sad house?

'So what about you?' she asked, desperate to turn the subject. 'Tell me about Bruce. Was that what the phone call on Thursday was about? You know, I now have a farm big enough for all of us. If you need me to foster him…'

'Are you kidding? Nico adores him. Nico was living in a campervan when he first arrived but he found this gorgeous house near the beach—well, actually I found it for him—and he and Bruce are living the dream. They're at the beach every day. Bruce just waits on the sand, watching like a hawk while Nico does his paddle-boarding thing.'

'And Bruce is okay? He wasn't as hurt as Stumpy?'

'He had a badly bruised, strained leg so he was bandaged up and limping for a while, but the main problem was psychological. He was really traumatised. If it hadn't been for the way he bonded with Nico and trusted him right from the start, I don't know how this would have played out. But don't worry. Nico's not going to let anything bad happen to him. And I don't think he'll be giving him up for adoption any time soon.'

'That's so good to hear. We never did find any relative or friend of Charlie's who could take the dogs. Now, tell me…'

But then Jen's phone pinged again and so did Frankie's. The rain was easing, the forecast looked okay and transfer was about to happen.

'Back to work,' Jen said ruefully as she gave her friend a final hug. 'Isn't it lucky we love our jobs? Sometimes it seems like work is time out for both of us.'

Rob arrived back at the hospital mid-morning on Monday, half an hour before the start of clinic. His visits to Brisbane were an established routine. He dropped Jacob off at childcare as he drove through town, then headed home for a quick shower and change.

He walked through the kitchen—and Jenny's mug was gone.

Maybe it was weird, to notice it as soon as he walked in the door, but it was quite some mug. It was an elephant, large and fat and fluorescent pink, with the trunk forming the handle. The grin on its cartoon-like face was one of pure glee.

'One of my patients gave me this,' she'd told Rob when she'd first produced it. 'Malcolm's nine years old now, but when he was seven he had non-Hodgkin's lymphoma. His mum was single and struggling, she didn't have a car and Malcolm was immunocompromised. We transferred him back and forth to hospital so many times we became friends, and the Christmas they announced he was clear he and his mum gave me this. There's no way this baby's going near any dishwasher.'

It had sat in pride of place next to his state-of-the-art coffee machine, and both he and Jacob had decided they liked it. A lot.

And now it was gone. Why did that make his heart sink?

Maybe she'd left it in her room. Instead of heading to his end of the house, to his room, he went to hers. Knocked.

Nothing.

It was mid Monday morning. Of course she wouldn't be here. He had no business looking.

But he looked—and there was no mug. Not only that, the room looked exactly as it had looked before she'd arrived.

Clean. Neat.

Empty.

There was a note on the bed addressed to him. He walked forward and picked it up.

> *Rob,*
> *Angus will probably tell you that Paul came to see me while you were away. Even before that, though, I was realising how impossible this situation is. So I guess I've decided that this is all getting too heavy, too fast. It might seem cowardly, and maybe it is, but Ruth needs someone to look after her farm and it seems a sensible solution for us all.*
>
> *I don't want to upset Jacob though, so maybe you could bring him to see the alpacas at the weekend? He'll like the farm.*
>
> *Welcome home, Rob, and take care of you.*

He stood and stared at the note for a long, long time and then slowly he crumpled it between his fingers. *How impossible this situation is.*

She had it in one. Impossible, impossible, impossible.

He thought of Paul coming to see her and he felt ill. The last four years of unrelenting grief had seen a once sensible, urbane lawyer inch closer and closer to the edge of reason. Rob understood, but what was happening now was past irrational. He could only guess what sort of anger had been thrown at Jen.

How could he hope that she withstood that? How could he ask her to?

He couldn't. He stood in the empty bedroom and he thought of their night together, what, only four nights ago? That night had felt like the heavens had opened, light, freedom—a future!—had suddenly seemed possible.

But it had been an illusion. The weekend, this note, was his reality. It was what it was, and he had no right to ask Jen to share.

What had she said in her note? *It might seem cowardly...* It wasn't cowardly, he thought. This grim reality was his, and he had no business to ask her to share.

He closed his eyes and for a moment he let despair wash over him. Emma was still a part of his life, and her parents' anger and distress were part of his life as well. To move on...to let the embryonic concept of Jen sharing his life when Emma was still real, still...loved?...what was he doing? What right did he have to want Jen to share?

He was feeling ill—the emotions in his head were so knotted that he had no chance of unravelling them—but a knock on the door brought him back to the here and now. Minnie stood in the doorway, her face a picture of concern.

'Oh, Rob,' she said miserably. And then, 'Let me make you a nice cup of tea.'

He raked his hair and then almost visibly braced.

'That'd be great, Minnie,' he told her. 'But I need to move fast. Clinic's in twenty minutes.'

'Pop in to see Anna before you go to clinic,' Minnie suggested. 'It'll make you a tiny bit late, but it'll be worth it.'

'Why?'

'Because Anna's happy and her baby's gorgeous,' Minnie said softly. 'Sometimes we all need to remind ourselves that happy ever after is possible.'

As if. But she gave him a hug as he passed, and somehow it helped.

So he showered and had his tea—and then he did what Minnie had suggested. He ducked into the hospital, to find Anna surrounded by soft toys, flowers, baby paraphernalia. Cuddling her baby. And when she saw Rob she smiled shyly and held out her son.

'Would you like a cuddle?'

And he would. He stood in the sunlit room and held a tiny newborn in his arms and remembered holding Jacob four years ago. And with that came memories of grief, of shock, but, superimposed, was the wonder and the surge of protectiveness and hope that had filled him at the sight of his little son.

This was what it was all about, he told himself. He loved Jacob so much and he still had to fight for him.

And what he felt for Jenny?

'It's not about me,' he whispered to this tiny scrap of snuggling infant. And then he looked at Anna and smiled.

'You're doing so well. He's beautiful, Anna.'

'He is, isn't he?' Anna told him, her smile shy but happy. 'Mum and Dad have said they'll help and that's wonderful—unbelievable even—but as soon as I saw him I knew... I can cope, even by myself if I have to. I'll do whatever it takes.'

'I know you will,' Rob told her. 'Don't we all?' And then he handed back her precious baby and headed to work.

Knowing he'd accept...whatever it took.

CHAPTER ELEVEN

THANKFULLY, AT LEAST for Jenny's state of mind, after that life got busy. Put simply, the heavens opened. The creek rose, flooding parks and playground. The sea became a swirling brown mass of foam as the inland water surged outward from the creek's mouth, creating a dirty brown bloom instead of the gorgeous sapphire surf Willhua was known for. The district became swathed in mud.

And that meant medical problems. The muggy heat meant beachgoers were tempted into the water regardless of warnings. There were cuts from debris, and infections caused by contaminated water.

There were minor car accidents as vehicles slipped on muddy roads. Two farm accidents where tractors had slid and rolled left one farmer with crushed ribs, another with a badly fractured leg. The mud in the farming community meant falls. Sodden boots led to infections, and a landslip between Willhua and Whale Head meant that Willhua's two doctors were coping with problems they'd normally have referred on to specialists in the larger town.

Jen and Gary were working flat out as well. The ambulance was four-wheel drive, bought with just such weather conditions in mind, and it was increasingly needed for almost trivial transfers. Olivia Hoffman's leg needed dressing, her intrepid daughter wasn't brave enough to face the winding road, but the filthy conditions meant that Hildy wasn't the only one to admit that they didn't feel confident and asked for the ambulance to collect them.

Rob and Jenny therefore saw each other only in passing, as patients were transferred in and out. Finally, though, the Saturday after he'd arrived home, the skies cleared a little.

'Please can we see Jen and Stumpy today?' a tearful Jacob pleaded. He'd been unutterably distressed to get home and find them gone— though Rob thought it was Stumpy he missed more than Jen. Maybe he should get a dog himself, he thought, but then he thought of Jen and Stumpy and thought, *One without the other?*

The thought was illogical, and it left him feeling desolate. Just do what comes next, he told himself. It was Saturday morning and for the first time all week he had time.

'Sure, I'm home.' Jen sounded cautious when he phoned, as well she might. But then she seemed to catch herself and her voice became enthusiastic. 'We have a baby alpaca. Jacob will love him.'

So he drove up to the small farm and Jen met them at the gate, swinging it open for them to drive through.

She looked like a farmer, he thought. She was wearing faded jeans, an oversized T-shirt and muddy gumboots. Her hair was flying every which way in the wind, and a large smear of mud lay across her cheek. She was smiling a greeting and waving to Jacob, and as Rob waited for her to swing the gate wide he was hit by a wave of longing so great it was all he could do not to groan out loud.

There was a sudden vision… A small farm, just like this. A big farmhouse kitchen. Dogs, kids, mess.

Family.

Jenny.

'Hey, are you awake in there?' She was holding the gate wide, he realised, waiting for him to go through, and he'd paused too long. He managed a grin and drove on. And then he had parked and Jacob was fighting to get his seatbelt undone, then clambering out of the car, across the muddy yard and into Jen's outstretched arms.

She stooped to catch him. She hugged and swung and laughed with his little son and there it was again. That surge of longing so great he could hardly bear it.

'Welcome to mud city,' she called to him. 'I hope you brought gumboots.'

He had. Luckily Jacob was already wearing his. That meant Jen's thighs were now liberally smeared with mud, but she didn't seem to care.

'Stumpy first, or alpacas?' she asked and motioned to the back door. There stood two dogs, Ruth's gorgeous collie, and Stumpy. They were both looking at Rob and Jacob, and looking dubiously at the mud.

'Smart dogs,' Jen said, chuckling at their expressions. 'They've learned every time they go out I put them in the outside shower and wash off their mud. It's either that or they stay outside for the day. Neither of them enjoys the experience, so they head out in the morning, get their running out of their system and then figure out whether any future excursion is worth the consequences. They're looking at you now and hoping if they wait long enough you'll come to them.'

'And they've fallen for each other,' she added. 'I reckon most of the reason Stumpy was miserable was that she was missing Charlie and Bruce. But now she's found Bosun and she has a new love. Fickle, thy name is Stumpy.'

She smiled again and swung Jacob around and set him on his feet, and Rob looked at her face, marred with mud but clear and open and happy, and he thought…he'd only known her for three weeks.

How could he fall so hard in three weeks?

But Jacob had met the dogs' expectations. He'd raced across to them and had his arms around Stumpy's neck and Stumpy was doing her best to lick every part of the small boy she obviously thought was her best friend in the world.

It was only three weeks since Stumpy had lost her owner, he thought, and then he thought that it wasn't just Stumpy who was fickle.

'Let's check out these alpacas before it starts raining again,' Jen was saying, and Jacob gave a final hug to Stumpy and came back to join them. The little boy took Jen's hand and held it like… like Jen was family.

'I've missed you,' Jacob said simply.

Jen said, 'I've missed you too.'

Gut wrench.

He followed the two of them into the stable. Most of the alpacas were in the adjoining paddock, soaking up the first glimpse of sun they'd seen for a week, but in one of the stalls was a white and tan-gold alpaca, and by her side was a newborn…foal?

'She's a cria,' Jen told them. 'That's what baby

alpacas are called, Jacob. She was born last night and we're very excited. I was up at midnight. I had to video call Ruth,' she told Rob. 'Ruth's already started chemo and she's very tired but there was no way she was going to sleep while this was happening. So Ruth supervised via video link and I followed her instructions, but in the end Betty did it all herself. Ruth's named this one Pamela. So meet Pamela, people. You're the first outside people she's met.'

'She's littler than me,' Jacob said, awed. 'Hi, Pamela.'

'When she's a little bit older you can pat her,' Jen told him.

'Not yet?' He looked up. 'Would she bite?'

'Alpacas don't bite,' she told him. 'They don't have any top teeth so they can't, and Betty's very tame. But Betty's only just met Pamela herself and this is her first baby. She's only just learning to love her baby herself, so we have to give her time and space.'

'Like me when Minnie gave me Eric-the-Scarecrow at my birthday party,' he said thoughtfully. 'I had to go into my bedroom all by myself 'cos I wasn't ready to share yet.'

'Exactly,' Jen said. 'But you know what you could do for her? See her water container? It's getting low. There's a trough outside but she's not ready to use that yet. There's a yellow bucket under the tap over there. Could you fill it, not too full, just enough for you to carry, and bring it over to tip into her bowl?'

'Yes!' Jacob said enthusiastically. 'Then they can both drink.' Then he looked doubtfully at Pamela, who was showing in a very elementary way her preferred beverage. 'But Pamela's drinking from her mummy.'

'And that's why Betty needs lots of water,' Jen told him. 'Mummies turn water into milk and that's how babies feed.'

'Yes,' Jacob said again and carefully handed Eric-the-Scarecrow to Rob and headed for the tap.

They watched as he trudged back and forth, taking his task very seriously. He filled the bucket to about a quarter, tested it, figured it was heavy enough, and carried it over. After the first careful trip Betty was obliging enough to drink. 'Yes!' Jacob crowed again and turned and high-fived Jen and then headed back, determined to fill the whole bowl.

Which left them alone—apart from Eric-the-Scarecrow.

What to say?

'I'm sorry you had to meet Paul,' Rob said at last, because it had to be said. And he could say it now, when he wasn't looking at her. They were both determinedly looking at Jacob.

'I'm sorry you need to cope with Paul,' she told him. 'I can see... I can see just how dreadful it is...for all you.'

'It is,' he said and went back to watching Jacob.

Where to take this from here? In her note she'd described this situation as impossible. It surely was.

'Jen, does it have to be all or nothing?' he asked at last, feeling that every word was somehow loaded. 'I know you've moved out and I can understand that, but could we... I don't know... have dinner, meet sometimes...?'

'We're meeting now.'

'You know what I mean,' he said, and then spread his hands. 'Hell, Jen, I know it's impossible, I know I have no right to ask, but I want more.'

'Rob, you're married.'

It was said almost in a whisper, but it sounded so loud it seemed to resonate, echoing almost up to the rafters and back. And then she turned and looked at him and what he saw there...he didn't know...but her face creased in distress.

'I'm sorry,' she said, her voice wobbling a bit. 'That sounds so hard, so unfair. You're married but not married. You're caught in an appalling bind, but me being with you... Rob, it can't help. It can surely only make things worse.'

'We could try. Face it down together.'

'It's too soon.' Then she shook her head. 'No, that's a lie. It's not too soon. And before you ask, I wasn't talking about the four years since you lost Emma. I was talking about the three weeks since I met you. How can I feel about you…the way I do…after three short weeks? Being honest… I have no idea. I only know that I do. But Rob, long or short, timely or not, I don't have the courage to take this further. I just…can't.'

And what was he to say to that?

Nothing, he thought bitterly. He had no right to ask anything of this woman. This was his tragedy, his world, and there was no justification to ask her to share.

Because it would be sharing, he thought. If Jen was to stand by him, then Paul and Lois's grief would be magnified a thousandfold. He knew it'd be directed at Jen, and there'd be no way he could stop it.

'Jacob, I've made scones,' Jen said, her voice carefully lightened, redirected into neutral territory. 'They're a bit wobbly but if we cover them with jam and cream maybe we won't notice the wobbles. But I'm trying to remember—should you put jam on first or cream? What do you think?'

'Jam,' Jacob said definitely. 'And then cream

and then more jam. Can Stumpy and Bosun have one?'

'Yes,' Jen said. 'You know, there are so many things in the world we can't have that I can't see that one scone will change a thing.'

They ate scones while Jen and Jacob talked and Rob said what was necessary, but only just. Then they drove away, and she was left with half a dozen wobbly scones and two dogs who'd like to eat more. As if on cue, the moment they drove out of the gate the rain started again in earnest.

Dammit. She almost wished her phone would ping, that there'd be a call from Gary. She didn't need time to think.

'Let's go for a walk,' she told the dogs, who eyed her dubiously. Yep, they knew about the shower. But once she was in her wet weather gear they decided enthusiasm was called for. So they headed out across the paddocks, checking on the outside alpacas, telling them they'd be much more comfortable in the stables, but a bit of rain didn't seem to be worrying them. Then they headed further.

The farm bordered the creek on its north side—or the river as it now was. The dogs headed off on a rabbit hunt and Jen was left staring at the swollen water. Calling herself all sorts of coward.

But how not to be?

Unbidden, thoughts of that awful night with Darren were flooding back. Frankie had told her she'd met his wife at the farewell function the service had put on before they'd returned to the States. According to Frankie, Darren's wife was a corporate high-flyer, but Frankie had said, the way she'd looked at Darren… Whatever arrangement they'd made where one worked in Australia, the other in New York, it was clear she adored him.

Two marriages. Two women married to men Jen thought…thought she loved?

'I can't cope with this.' She was talking out loud but the torrent of water rushing past was drowning her speech, making it personal. As it was meant to. Her conscience talking to her heart?

'I have to stay strong,' she whispered. 'I'm only here for two more months. I need to do what I came for and then get out of their lives.

'You *are* a coward.'

'I might be,' she said bleakly and then, 'Okay, I am. But the alternative…the vitriol I'd bring down on all our heads…the hurt…'

She couldn't do it.

She turned and headed back to the house, and

if the rain on her face was mingling with tears there was no one to see.

'Which is just as well,' she whispered. 'The last thing Rob needs is more hurt.'

CHAPTER TWELVE

IT RAINED. IT rained and it rained and it rained, which pretty much suited Jenny's mood.

It also meant that she and Gary were as busy as they were likely to be. Their well-equipped ambulance—four-wheel drive, built with a high chassis to cope with the rough inland roads—became almost a normal mode of public transport.

Angus was called back in from his veggie garden—it was too sodden to work there anyway—and he and Rob were run off their feet. Many of the district's elderly residents were too fearful to face the appalling weather conditions. If they lived close by, either Rob or Angus did house calls. If not, Gary and Jen brought patients to the surgery.

Between work and the demands of the dogs and the alpacas, Jen scarcely had time to think—except she did think. The week that followed Rob and Jacob's visit she felt probably more desolate than she'd ever felt in her life.

'But there's nothing I can do about it,' she told herself, but a little voice nagged back... *If you had courage...*

It was doing her head in—and then there was a drama that pretty much drove even heartbreaking thoughts from her mind.

High in the hills, almost fifty kilometres from Willhua, was a dam, a massive man-made holding pond for millions of litres of water. It had been built to supply almost all of Southern Sydney with drinking water. An unseasonably wet summer had seen it fill to almost capacity, and now, with these unrelenting rains, it was close to overflowing.

The powers that be had been monitoring the situation, allowing enough water to escape to alleviate pressure on the dam walls. But on the Thursday and Friday after the farm visit a weather front passed that was so severe the water topped the dam wall.

The wall wasn't built for such pressure. The authorities panicked and set release to maximum but, with the water already at flood levels below the dam, the scenario was disastrous.

There was nowhere for the water to go. The colossal discharge probably avoided a greater catastrophe, the bursting of the dam wall, but even this... It meant a massive wave of water surged along the already water-soaked valley, sweeping all before it.

Jen got the call at midnight and Gary sounded terrified. 'Every boat, every kayak, every able-bodied person who can man them… Jen, heaven knows what we're facing.'

What followed was a massive community effort to reach outlying properties, to make sure people were safe. There were also casualties, people taking risks to move stock, to save belongings, to cope with a situation none had envisaged. There were fractures, lacerations, hysteria and paralysing shock as residents saw their homes filled with debris-laden water.

As Jen worked throughout the night and well into the next day, she was aware that her former crew, with Frankie on board, was in the skies helping with evacuations. There was no time for chat, though. Neither was there time for talk with Rob—patients were handed over fast so she and Gary could get out there again.

She would have preferred some other way of giving herself some head space from the personal.

'It puts things in perspective,' she told herself as she and Gary treated a young mum who'd sliced her foot heading back into a flooded house trying to find her kid's beloved teddy.

As she worked, she was reminded of Jacob and Eric-the-Scarecrow. Rob would have done the same, she thought, if Eric had been at risk. He loved his son so much. He'd do...whatever it took.

He had done whatever it took. He'd accepted a life of isolation.

But then the next call came in, and she had to abandon the pointless thoughts that kept drifting into her head at unwanted moments. There was only flood and drama, and if that meant a little time out from the way her head was working... well, she'd accept it.

She just needed to get on.

And then, mid-afternoon, came drama that almost drove everything else out of her mind.

The call was to an outlying farm. The road there was still clear, but only just. Access to the property was via a narrow track, a raised strip of gravel surrounded on all sides by lakes that would normally be bushland or paddocks. In parts, the water was sloshing over.

The call, passed on by emergency services, said simply that a woman was in labour. As they drove they could see why the couple had elected to call the four-wheel drive ambulance rather than risk driving to hospital themselves.

But when they reached the farmhouse they found a young man alone, standing on the veranda, looking frantic. He looked soaked to the skin, he was wearing shorts and T-shirt and had bare feet, and on his leg was a long, jagged cut, bleeding sluggishly.

But he wasn't worried about his leg.

'I wanted a boat,' he screamed at them as they pulled up in the driveway. 'I told them, I need a boat. Or a helicopter. The wind's coming up. It's getting worse and my wife's stuck. Where's the boat?'

'Mate, slow down a little and tell us where she is.' Gary's voice was calm and authoritative, imbued with years of experience in times of crisis.

'She's at our place.'

'And where's your place?'

'Along the creek.' The man was sobbing with fear and frustration, but Gary's gaze held his and he managed to choke back his terror enough to talk. 'The water came. That was okay, our house seemed high and Skye said she didn't want to evacuate. She wants a home birth. We've got it all organised, a birth pool set up in the living room, two midwives booked to come. And she's not due till Saturday. So we stayed put and then this wave hit. The water's all through the bottom floor, almost to ceiling height. Everything's flooded. We have kayaks, just little ones, but the water's crazy. And then…then Skye started having pains.'

'So she's still at your house?' Gary's voice was calm, refusing to buy in to the young man's panic.

'My phone wouldn't work. The electrics are out. I dunno how that's affecting transmission but I knew Gareth…he owns this place…has a landline and he has a decent boat. He takes it out fishing from Willhua. I thought I'd get here and call for help and we'd both go back and get her. But Gareth's gone and so has his boat. I guess he'll be using it to move stock—I dunno. At least I could ring though, but they put me through to the ambulance. But I didn't want the ambulance. I want someone to reach Skye.'

Gary nodded. 'Okay, mate, let's see what we can do. Jen, you contact headquarters. Meanwhile…' He looked down at the man's leg. 'Let's get this seen to.'

'My wife!' The guy backed as if they were about to arrest him. 'Don't you understand? She's by herself. In that house. And the water's getting higher.'

But Jen was already on the radio, and what she heard there made her heart sink. With evacuations all across the valley there was no one close enough to help. No boats. No choppers. The control room dispatcher sounded close to tears herself.

'I'll get a crew there as soon as I can,' she

promised. 'But honestly, I don't know when that'll be.'

'A woman alone in labour surely takes precedence.'

'We have people on roofs of houses that seem in danger of collapsing. Is there no way you can get there yourself?'

While Gary tended the young man's leg, calming him, gently questioning—Were there any other children? How far advanced was his wife's labour? How far apart were the pains?—Jen looked out of the window at the driving rain. The water seemed to be rising while she watched, and so was the wind. She thought that if the ground floor of the house had been flooded hours ago, how much worse would it be now?

We have people on roofs of houses in danger of collapsing... A woman alone in labour...

But, pulled up under a dry patch of land under the picture windows of the house she was in, lay a kayak, bright crimson, built for one.

There lay a possibility.

She turned back to Gary and the man—Douglas—Gary had got that out of him. 'Is that your kayak?' she asked.

'I...yes. That's how I got here. We have two but there was no way Skye could use hers.'

At nine months pregnant? Thank heaven she didn't try.

'So where's your house?' she asked. 'Upstream or downstream?' If it was upstream, with the ever-increasing strength of wind and water, she wouldn't have a chance.

'I…it's downstream. That's why it took so long to get here. I had to fight the current and it was getting stronger by the minute. I'm strong but this was something else. I went through the bush at the water's edge to avoid the worst, paddled and waded when I had to. That's how I ripped my leg.'

And you were wearing shorts and thongs, Jen thought, but she didn't say so. She was thinking ahead, thankfully, of the tough cloth her uniform was made of, and of her workmanlike boots.

'But the bush wasn't so dense to stop you getting through?' she asked.

'Jen…' Gary said uneasily, seeing where she was going. 'You can't.'

She met his gaze head-on. 'A woman alone, in labour… If you were thirty years younger, would you do it?' she asked.

They stared at each other for a long, long moment. Then Gary said at last, heavily, 'Don't tell me. You've used kayaks since you were two?'

'I used to compete in white-water rafting.'

'Of course you did.'

She chuckled. 'There you go, then. You really should have read my résumé.'

But Douglas was staring from one to the other, his face ashen. 'What are you suggesting? If anyone tries to get back it has to be me.'

'Jen has a satellite radio, plus medical equipment, plus medical skills,' Gary said. 'Mate, there's no contest. You called us for a reason. But Jen, you know how dangerous…'

'I won't take risks,' she promised, untruthfully but they both knew that. 'If I stay in the bush as much as possible, I'll just be fighting my way from tree to tree. I promise I won't try and ride the current. Douglas, where exactly is your house?'

'You can see the roof.' He pointed downstream and they saw the glint of a metal roof, far off through the rain.

'Then I'm wasting time being here. Worst case scenario is that I get stuck, climb a decent tree, radio for help and wait for a chopper to come get me. But if that happens tell them to reach Skye first, because I'm good at clinging to trees and these gums are solid. I could stay there till morning if need be. Gary, if I get stuck, talk to Frankie at South Sydney Air Rescue. She'll give me an earful but she'll rescue me.'

'I'll contact Doc Pierson,' Gary said uneasily. 'He'll…'

'This is nothing to do with Rob,' she told him,

almost harshly. 'He'll be up to his ears in his own work.'

'Oh, Jen...'

'Hey, don't fret,' she said and on impulse she leaned forward and hugged him. 'He travels the fastest who travels alone.'

'That pronoun should be *she*,' Gary said morosely. 'Bloody independent women!'

Dusk.

The South Sydney Air Rescue chopper landed on the stretch of land behind the hospital. Normally they used the oval but it, too, was underwater. Frankie helped the little family down. They'd been perched on a rooftop for hours, they were cold and wet and traumatised but Willhua had organised itself. Volunteers received them with blankets, warmth and reassurance, and within moments they were heading into the security of the school hall-cum-evacuation centre.

But Frankie was heading into the hospital at a run.

Rob met her in the entrance. He and Angus had worked steadily all day, but the stream of medical events seemed to have eased. One look at Frankie's face though, and he knew there was more.

'You're Dr Pierson, right?' she demanded, wasting no time.

'Right.'

'I'm Frankie. South Sydney Air Rescue. Friend of Jen's. Doctor, is it possible for you to leave here?' she asked. 'Do you have cover? And before you answer, would you be prepared to be dropped into a home visit? Jen and Gary were called out earlier to a woman in labour. Skye Robbins—do you know her?'

He did know her, and his heart sank. Skye had been seeing him for antenatal care, but she'd come to him reluctantly, only at the insistence of her midwives. She'd been intent on a home birth from the start, and now... He thought of the isolation of their small farm and he felt ill.

Frankie was watching his face—guessing his reaction? 'So you know her? She's alone, trapped in a house with a flooded ground floor. Her husband kayaked out to get help, but now the water's risen further, leaving her isolated. When the ambulance couldn't reach her Jen kayaked in by herself.

'No, don't look like that,' she said as he stared at her in dismay. 'I know you're a friend of Jen. Yes, she's crazy, but that's why we love her, and she's one of the most capable women I know. She told you she's a trained nurse? Anyway, she and her expectant mum have been waiting on evac for hours, but there's been so much need. There's still need. Now Jen's radioed in saying she's worried about progress, but there's nowhere we can land. She needs... well, to put it bluntly, she needs you. I'd have to take you down in a harness attached to mine, but I'd make sure you're safe. Could you come?'

Could he?

Angus could cope here, he thought, his mind in overdrive. Minnie had been staying with Jacob for the last two days, so that was fine, but what would he be facing? He was no obstetrician. Willhua's mums usually went to Whale Head to deliver. Even Anna's birth had been unusual.

'What does she say about progress?'

'Second stage, but no progress for hours—Jen's worrying about obstructed labour. Without obstruction, the birth could happen at any minute but she's becoming more and more distressed.'

And with that came a flood of possible diagnoses. He thought of what he knew of Skye. She was a small woman, finely boned. He'd done an ultrasound six weeks ago and things had looked normal, but the baby's head grew fast in the last weeks of pregnancy. Cephalopelvic proportion couldn't normally be diagnosed before the thirty-seventh week because the baby's head wouldn't have reached birth size. If Skye's pelvis was simply too small... What a nightmare.

'We have to get her out,' he said flatly. 'If she needs a Caesarean...'

'Let's hope it won't come to that,' Frankie said grimly. 'This weather's getting worse. There's no second-floor balcony, no easy way we can lift from the house, and it's possible that she'll be too close to delivering to be moved by the time we get there. The crew's consensus is the best we can do is provide additional medical assistance, but we need to do it now. Jen thinks the woman's in real trouble and she wouldn't say it lightly.'

'She needs an obstetrician.'

'We've looked at options. Even if we manage to find one willing, the nearest specialist is at Whale Head. With the dark and rising wind it'll be impossible to get anyone but you there. You could talk to them via satellite phone but that's the best we can do. Please, can you help?'

His mind was almost spinning. With no power, with no theatre equipment, there was no possibility of a Caesarean. If she'd been in second stage for hours...if the pressure stayed on...the prospect was hellish. Even if the baby died, the threats wouldn't end. There could be rupture, maybe even maternal death. He'd be fighting for Skye's life as well.

'We can drop gear with you,' Frankie said diffidently. 'Lanterns, equipment, you name it.'

'You know I can't do a Caesar in the conditions you describe.' Even if he had expert advice via the satellite phone, in this situation he knew his limitations.

'We figured that,' Frankie told him. 'So the situation's grim but we don't want it to be...' She stopped, unable to voice the unthinkable. 'Doctor, we don't want Jen to be on her own, so the more medical expertise we can get in there, the better. We said we'd try. Jen's had a look and suggested a dry place where someone—you?—can be dropped, and she's figuring a system to get you into the house.'

'Of course she has,' Rob said, and Frankie managed a wry grin.

'You know our Jen, then.'

'I surely do.'

He thought of her, kayaking into floodwaters on her own. Stranded with a woman giving birth. Facing obstructed labour, knowing the ramifications but moving to the practical. Figuring out systems to get gear into a flooded house.

Yes, he knew Jen.

He would have gone anyway. There was no choice—but this was Jen.

And with that thought came another, so heavy and strong and sure that it almost blindsided him.

Somehow he had to know her better.

* * *

'Rob's coming.' Frankie's voice on the radio seemed a lifeline all in itself.

'Who?'

'Your Doc Pierson, of course. Can I put you through to the boys to tell them where we can set him down?'

'Yeah,' she said, dazed. 'But… Rob?'

'You said you needed help,' Frankie told her and, for heaven's sake, she heard a trace of humour in her friend's voice. 'A trained obstetrician's our first choice, but that's impossible. Second choice should surely be me,' she added with mock modesty. 'You know I'd be brilliant, but I'm needed with the crew. So, for some reason, the crew and I decided your Doc Pierson would be better.'

'*My* Doc Pierson?'

'You should have seen his face when I told him you'd kayaked in,' Frankie said. 'If he's not your Doc Pierson, I'm a monkey's uncle.'

Maybe he should have spent all the time he had during the short flight to keep reviewing everything he knew about obstructed labour. Those thoughts had been front and centre back at the hospital, while he and Angus had swiftly put together everything they could think of he might need. Now, in the back of the darkened chopper, he had moments to take a breath, ready himself for descent...and think of something apart from medical need.

His thoughts were of Jen, on her own, fighting for a woman's life, doing what she did best. But then, as he watched the swirling mass of floodwater below them, illuminated by the chopper's floodlights, he also thought...what about Jacob?

Minnie was caring for him. Right now Jacob was fine, but if something happened...

He was being winched down to a tiny area of dry land above a flooded house. Frankie had described it to him—apparently they'd flown over it on their way to drop the little family they'd just rescued. Fully loaded, they hadn't been able to do anything, but they'd had time to look.

'The house is two-storey,' she'd told him. 'The bottom level's underwater, but the second storey's still above water level. There's a rise at the back of the house, where they usually park an old tractor which, fortunately, isn't there at the moment. It's too small to land but it looks safe enough to winch you down. It's a short distance to the house and Jen says she's organising a rope system from the other end to get you safely across.'

She'd hesitated, and then added, 'Rob, there are risks. We shouldn't ask this of you but...'

'But lives are at stake,' he'd said, and he'd known there was no choice.

But, sitting in the darkened chopper, reminding himself of the instructions Frankie had given him, the choice he'd made was suddenly not so clear.

This crew was incredibly capable. He knew that, but a night descent in the wind…appalling things could happen. And if anything happened to him, where would that leave Jacob? Up until now he hadn't had room for the thought, but now it was like a wave of black, a terror that left him almost immobilised.

But then, suddenly, weirdly, into this kaleidoscope of racing need, he was thinking of Emma. He was remembering Em's laughter, her love, her joy in her pregnancy, her anticipation of her coming baby. This was another baby he was fighting for. Em had trained as a doctor for a reason, and he knew what she'd say:

A mum and a baby? What's the risk compared to the outcome?

And then he was thinking again of Jen, who'd kayaked alone into a flooded house. Jen was doing what she must to help a woman in labour, a terrified woman.

His thoughts were so tangled, but superimposing themselves in his mind now were other images. Jen hugging Stumpy, declaring she'd keep her. Jen climbing the chain tepee with Jacob at the playground. Jen in his kitchen, making Jacob laugh, making him laugh.

As Em would have made Jacob laugh.

Emma and Jenny.

Two women he loved.

What's the risk compared to the outcome?

And, for some reason, as he sat in the noise-filled rear of the chopper, readying himself to descend, the fog of grief and anger and helplessness of the last four years seemed to clear.

For all these years he'd been grieving for Emma, but at the same time he'd felt as if he'd been walking on eggshells. He'd been trying to placate Lois and Paul, trying to do everything he could to ensure they had no legal means of contesting custody.

And now... If he died tonight they'd gain custody, but he'd faced that risk almost without thinking—because lives were at stake.

And then he thought—what was at stake if he didn't fight for Jen?

He thought of Tony, driving his appalling black car, constantly watching them. He'd accepted it as just...what was.

He was thinking of his living room, a place both he and Jacob hated. A shrine to Emma. Emma would have loathed it.

And now there was Jenny—or the chance

of Jenny. He thought of her courage, her sheer love of life. Of the way she'd lifted the fog of grief that had shrouded his home. Of the way she'd seamlessly accepted the responsibility of Stumpy. Of the way she'd made his little son laugh.

And then…of the way her body had melted into his, of the way she'd shown him the vibrant, passionate woman she could be.

Why had he calmly accepted her decision to move out? The answer was simple.

Because what was left after four long years was dreary acceptance of reality.

But then…tonight? Tonight he was risking everything because he could save lives. But by not risking…what sort of lives were he and Jacob to lead?

'We're ready to move to the door.' Frankie was checking the carabiner that attached Rob's harness to her own. 'You want me to go through things one more time?'

'No, I have it.'

'You're sure?'

'I'm sure,' he told her, shaking off introspection and centring himself on what had to be done. The door of the chopper was open. Rob was securely attached and would be until his feet were safely on the patch of ground now illuminated by the powerful light beneath the helicopter. Then he would be unclipped and remove his harness and Frankie would be winched back to the hovering aircraft. It sounded simple. It didn't feel simple.

But now, strangely, the perils of descent were overshadowed by thoughts of risks of another kind.

Risks…

Paul and Lois loved Jacob—he knew they did. If anything happened to him he'd have to trust that love would finally bring sanity to their care.

And there was another bottom line. He loved Jen, it was as straight and simple as that.

Maybe some risks had to be faced.

CHAPTER THIRTEEN

JEN HEARD THE approaching chopper above the wind, and she'd never been more grateful. Skye had been gripping her hand so tightly that she couldn't move, but the moment the contraction passed Jen was hanging out of the window, waving the torch that hung habitually on her equipment belt, to show the chopper where she was.

And then she saw them, two figures harnessed together, swinging down onto the top of the slope above the flooded house. The scene was lit by the chopper's searchlight. A gust of wind caught them and they swayed so close to the trees that she felt ill, and when they reached the ground she was almost dizzy with relief.

She saw the figures separate, then Frankie unclipped a back pack full of gear and handed it to Rob.

Rob…

'Skye, the doctor's here,' she told the woman on the bed behind her. 'He's brought everything we need, including pain relief.' That was the thing Skye wanted most. What Jen didn't tell her was that the bag Rob and Frankie were manoeuvring hopefully also contained other gear. She hadn't mentioned that to Skye, because what was the use in telling her what was happening wasn't normal when there wasn't a thing she could do about it? Skye had moved into second stage too long ago, and nothing was happening.

But now...

'He's coming in,' she told her, and Skye moaned.

'Be quick. Jen, please...'

But she didn't need to tell Jen to be quick— and Jen was ready.

Earlier, in between contractions, Skye had been able to answer questions, telling her what was where, and she'd had time to organise. She'd thus used Skye's kayak to get to the shed at the rear of the house, where she'd found nylon rope, luckily looped over high hooks, which meant it was above water level. 'The iron roof on the shed lifted during a storm last year,' Skye had told her. 'Douglas bought enough rope to tie it down until we could get a roofer in, and the rope should still be there.'

She'd got soaked reaching the rope and she'd decided to organise the whole thing while she was wet. So she'd waded and used the kayak, and managed to loop the rope, forming a circuit from her upper floor window to a tree near where someone could land.

When she'd got back to the house she'd attached the kayak to her makeshift pulley and sent it back to the drop site. And told Frankie. Who'd obviously told Rob.

Frankie was being winched up again. What other emergencies were Frankie and her crew facing tonight? How many other dramas were being played out across the state?

She could only focus on one.

She watched as Rob loaded gear into the kayak and started it on its way on its makeshift pulley. From above, the chopper's searchlight still lit the scene.

She had to focus. Rob had obviously figured her system, but they had to use it with care. The wind and the blast from the chopper was making the kayak sway. The last thing they needed was for the kayak to be snagged or tip halfway, and the fact that they were working in the dark didn't help.

But the gear arrived safely. She hauled it in with speed, then sent the kayak back.

Five minutes later Rob was clambering over the windowsill, into the room.

She didn't hug him. It would surely be inappropriate. They were medics on a job, and Skye, lying on the bed, recovering from her last contraction, had to see them as professionals. But as he'd stepped over the sill his hand had caught hers and held, and his grip said the idea of a hug wasn't all one-sided.

And then he was at the bed and professionalism was kicking in. 'Hey, Skye.' He caught the expectant mother's hands and Jen saw Skye's terror almost ease. 'I guess you've got your wish. Home birth after all.' His eyes were kind, his words strong and reassuring. 'Jen says you've been doing brilliantly.'

'It…hurts…'

'I'll bet it does. Mums have told me it's like pooing a pumpkin, and a big one at that. If you asked men to do that…well, women are awesome. But I can help now, and the chopper crew brought gear and drugs to give you some pain relief. We have some decent lamps. Let's get this place set up fast and then, if it's okay, I'll examine you.'

'I wanted a water birth.' Somehow Skye found the strength to wail. 'We've got a pool downstairs, all ready.'

Rob chuckled and his hand gripped hers again. 'So you told me. You said you've always wished for a water birth, but Skye, maybe you wished too hard. If we took you downstairs Jen and I would need to don snorkel and mask to deliver.'

And Skye even managed to smile back before the next contraction hit and she went back to focusing on getting this baby out.

Nothing else mattered but medical need. Skye knew Rob, he was her family doctor and his arrival seemed to give her strength, but her contractions were achieving nothing.

Rob, though, was moving swiftly. He was talking to Skye, asking permission for examination, telling her how far she was dilated, telling her that her baby's heartbeat was still steady. Not telling her what Jen had already told Frankie, and what she'd confirmed with him quietly as he'd entered—that labour hadn't progressed for hours.

And then, examination complete, he produced an ultrasound machine. Jen's knees almost sagged with relief as she saw him lift the appliance from its bag. A portable, state-of-the-art, battery-operated ultrasound seemed a game-changer. To be able to see what was happening…

But seeing wasn't fixing. One of the most common causes of obstructed labour was pelvic size, and if that was the case there was no way either of them could help, not here. And for Skye to continue labouring until first light, until conditions made evacuation possible… It didn't bear thinking of.

So all Jen could do was hold her breath and hold Skye's hand—Jen's hand was already painful from the death grip Skye had administered during contractions—and wait as Rob passed the wand over the swollen abdomen.

The silence seemed to go on for ever. The screen was so small Jen could hardly see the grainy image, so all she could do was keep on holding her breath. The world seemed to still. *Please*...

Maybe she was gripping Skye's hand too hard, returning pressure. She forced herself to loosen her hold but Skye grabbed her harder.

Both women were waiting for a verdict.

And then Rob's face changed, just a little. Just enough to give Jen hope.

'Skye, your bladder's full,' he said, calmly, as if this were an everyday occurrence, not something to shout from the rooftops. 'I'm looking at what's happening and I'm seeing your bladder's so full your baby can't get past it.'

'My bladder...' Skye whispered, confused.

'When did you last have a wee?'

'I couldn't,' she gasped. 'I mean...the toilet's downstairs. It's not working and last time... And I never even felt like I needed to.'

Dear God... Rookie mistake, Jen thought savagely. An empty bladder made for a safer delivery.

'It probably blocked early,' Rob said, cutting across Jen's instant self-blame. 'The fear from the flooding, plus early labour pains, plus no toilet…'

'But I don't think… I can't go now.'

'Because your baby's pushing so hard that everything's swollen.' He sounded prosaic but Jen heard the slight lift in his voice, a sign of hope. 'If it's okay with you, I'm going to insert a catheter. It's a simple procedure to drain the bladder and give bub room to move.'

'But I don't think I can push any more,' Skye moaned, and Rob moved so he could take her other hand.

'Women are awesome,' he told her again. 'Your baby's close and once your bladder's empty your body will take over. Skye, you have so much strength and you've done the hard yards. You have a baby in there who's aching to meet you, so let's make this happen.'

It sounded easy but it wasn't—inserting a catheter when things were so swollen and distended. Jen organised lighting, laid instruments out on sterile towels—catheter, forceps, just in case, and then set up a saline drip while Rob worked. And all the time Rob spoke to Skye gently, telling her what was happening, taking the terror out of the room.

He was taking terror out of Jen's mind as well. She'd been facing a night of Skye's continued obstructed labour, she'd known the probable outcome and it wasn't pretty. But now she was part of a capable, skilled team. Rob was here.

Maybe she'd have felt like this with any doctor—she'd certainly have been relieved—but this was Rob, with his kind eyes, his big, capable hands, his caring...

He and Emma had come to Willhua because they'd wanted to be family doctors, she thought, and it showed. Rob's compassion, his care, his skill were never more on show than they were tonight.

And, strangely, as she worked she was thinking of Emma. Until now Emma had seemed a ghostly entity, Rob's past, but their decision to be part of this community had been shared. If Emma had been here now...

For the first time she totally got the immensity of Rob's loss, his helplessness, his grief, and for the life of her she couldn't prevent her eyes welling. It was only for a moment though because...

Because the bladder emptied with a rush and almost instantly another contraction took over. The strength of it stunned them all. Skye was arching and screaming and her fingernails were digging into Jen's hand...

'Crowning,' Rob said, cutting across the

scream. 'Skye, here's the head, your baby's right here, one more hard, strong push—give it all you've got.'

And in the end it was almost a textbook-perfect birth. There was even time, as Rob placed the tiny newborn infant on Skye's breast, as Skye's hands cradled her new little daughter for the first time, as her face creased into wonder and love, for Jen to blink back more tears and then find her phone and take a video.

There was no phone reception—she couldn't send this—but by now Douglas would be beyond frantic. They could radio him the news. They could organise for Skye to talk to him, but in the end she knew this amateurish shot of the birth scene might become a treasure and it was important enough to make the time to get it right. She even swung around and pointed her phone out across the moonlit water, and then back to the bed. This birth could end up as family folklore.

And then she moved back into nurse mode, making sure mum and bub were warm, assisting Rob with a swift stitching—there'd been a slight tear—clearing the afterbirth.

'We thought,' Skye whispered as they worked around her, 'that we could plant the placenta under a rose bush.'

'Hmm.' Jen glanced out again at the moonlit night. The rain had eased and she could see the swirling water surrounding the house. 'Rose bushes? Tricky. And I'm betting your freezer's downstairs and flooded as well. Don't you have a nice big houseplant we could use instead?'

And Skye giggled and it was the best sound Jen thought she'd ever heard. The best!

Then there were calls to an almost hysterically relieved Douglas, to the chopper crew, and to Angus. Jen left that to Rob—he deserved that pleasure. She had enough to do.

The linen cupboard was upstairs and Jen found clean sheets. She managed to give Skye an almost-wash—it seemed there was an uncontaminated water tank connected to an upstairs tap! Then she helped Skye's first miraculous feed, she settled her into her clean bed with her baby cradled next to her and she watched them fall into a natural, blessedly peaceful sleep.

When finally she turned to Rob her heart was full. They'd turned down the lanterns. Rob was standing beside the bed, soaking up the sight of a sleeping mum and baby.

'It's a miracle,' she whispered.

'It is.'

'Emma would be so proud of you.' Where that had come from she didn't know, but she did know it for the truth. And she watched Rob's expression change.

'I think… I hope…'

'I know,' she said, definitely now. 'And yes, I never met her, but I know she left Sydney to be a country doctor and I can see her in those lovely pictures you have in your kitchen. Not the ones in the living room—the formal ones. Just the ones that say she loved being here, she loved what you were doing, and she loved you.'

'I can't...' He spread his hands helplessly and she took them.

'I'm not asking you to,' she told him. 'I wouldn't.'

'Jen...' There was stillness in the room. Even the whistling of the wind around the house seemed to have ceased. He held her hands, just held, as if he was fighting in his head for the next words. For the right words.

'Jenny, I'm still married to Em,' he said at last. 'She and I were partners in every sense, and I vowed to love and honour her until death do us part.'

'I know that,' she said, because something about this night had made her understand in a way she'd never understood before. The sight of him being winched down in wind and rain... The way he'd talked to Skye... The way he'd touched her baby's cheek, the tenderness, the awe...

This man was who he was...and she couldn't ask him to be any other way.

'Would it be wrong though?' he asked, and she could feel some of the tension of the night's drama surge back. 'Would it be so wrong to make those same vows to you? Because I've been thinking…tonight, no, longer, maybe for a month now… Jen, could I love and honour Emma, could I care for her until the end…but still…find a place for us? Because…' He released her hands and stood back a little, as if giving her space. Giving them both space for the momentous? 'I know it's not fair on you, but Jen, I do love you.'

And then there was silence, for so long that Jen thought she'd forgotten how to breathe. Maybe the whole world had forgotten how to breathe.

And then, finally, Jen said what must be said.

'Rob, isn't there something in those vows about forsaking all others? Would that do your head in?'

'Yeah,' he said and then he shook his head. 'Actually, I don't think we said that, but never mind. Because forsaking all others…who would that include? Jacob? Angus, Cathy, Gary, maybe the whole population of Willhua? Everyone I care about? I love Em, but I love so many more. And especially I love you. Jen, you know that I'm married. I can't divorce Em—and that's not because of Lois and Paul, it's because of me.

But I would be honoured, humbled, overjoyed, if you'd share my life in every other way.'

And Jen stood in the darkened bedroom, Skye and her baby were sleeping soundly on the bed nearby, water was lapping just underneath the floorboards, the rain was starting up again, and she thought…marriage.

She thought of Darren, standing in that opulent hotel room—was it only months ago?—with his stupid, shameful belligerence. *'I'm married. And my wife is here.'*

She'd been humiliated to her socks, but yet here was another man standing before her saying, *'I'm married.'*

It was so different. It was wonderfully, miraculously different.

Because she believed him. She trusted him. This was an honourable man and part of his honour was his love for Emma.

She thought back to that appalling scene in the kitchen. Of Paul's almost irrational anger. Of her decision that she lacked the courage to face this situation head-on.

But now…would it take so much courage to face this situation together—to face it side by side with the man she loved?

Because she did love him. She looked up into his beloved face, his anxious eyes, his gorgeous,

gorgeous self, and she thought—what gift is this that he's offering? To love me?

Loyalty showed itself in many guises, she thought, and this man had shown it in spades. To have such a man hold her, to give her a place in his life... What would she be thinking not to accept such a gift?

And all she needed was the courage to trust. The belief that this impossible situation was possible.

The acceptance of being loved, and loving in return.

'It'd have to include Stumpy,' she managed, because emotion was threating to overwhelm her and she somehow had to be prosaic. 'And...and Bruce too, if it doesn't work out with Frankie's mate, Nico. And I've promised to stay at the farm until Ruth comes back.'

'How could I ask you to break a promise?' His eyes were caressing her, holding her in thrall. 'Jen, I'm asking if our lives could merge, not one life dissolve into another's needs. I'll face down Lois and Paul...'

'You will not,' she said, suddenly on firm ground. 'Not by yourself. They're ours to deal with now.'

'They'll fight. They have all the legal...'

'And we have all the social,' she retorted. 'I haven't been a nurse and a paramedic for years for nothing. We don't need legal, we need social workers and psychologists and welfare workers. If needed, I could name a score who'd come into any court your in-laws choose and tell the judge just what this situation's doing to Jacob. That doesn't mean that Emma's not his mum, though,' she said. 'But maybe the Brisbane trips could be… I don't know. Different? Maybe even fun. Maybe we could take stuff there, decorate Emma's room, tell her fun stuff we've been doing. And then bookend the visits with zoo trips, or… I don't know…playing Pooh Sticks in the park? But it's *we*, Rob, because Emma's part of your life so I'm thinking she needs to be part of mine as well.'

'You've thought of this…'

'Not this minute,' she said, suddenly unsure again. 'But I've been at Ruth's for two weeks and I've been missing you so much.'

And why did that make him let go of her hands and kiss her, deeply and strongly, and then, because in this moment kissing wasn't enough, pick her up and whirl her round in the darkened bedroom? Finally they remembered where they were, that there was a sleeping new mum and her bub close by. But Skye and her baby were so deeply asleep that nothing could disturb them.

'You know,' Jen said thoughtfully as finally

Rob set her down, 'there are three bedrooms on this floor.'

'Really?'

'Really,' she told him. 'And one's just across the hall. If we left both doors open...'

'We could be dutiful medics, on duty all night,' Rob said and swung her up again, cradling her against his chest as if she weighed nothing. 'I'm a very light sleeper and, after all, staying in here might eventually disturb them.'

'I can set my watch timer for checks,' she told him.

'So you can. And if she calls or bub cries we'll be here in a flash.'

'We do need to sleep,' Jen said, smiling and smiling.

'So we do,' Rob replied, and she'd remember the smile he gave her then for the rest of her life. 'Eventually.'

At eight the next morning, when the rain had ceased and the wind had eased to practically nothing, a flat-bottomed Emergency Services boat reached the house. The crew on board roped it to the upper floor, 'Ahoy' rang out—but there was no instant reply.

Finally, though, a window was thrown open and a tousled-looking doctor in a shirt that wasn't quite buttoned leaned out.

'Hey,' one of the crew called. 'You guys need rescuing?'

'If we must,' he said obscurely and grinned. 'No. You're very welcome. There's a new baby here who needs to meet her dad.'

'Douglas is climbing walls.' The burly guy in charge, dressed in filthy yellow all-weather gear, was grinning back. 'So all's well?'

'All's well. Can you give us ten minutes to be respectable?'

'Glad to oblige,' the man said. 'We're set up to receive a stretcher. Are mum and bub stable?'

'I don't want her climbing out of windows but yes, things are fine. We're even dry.'

'Great.' The whole crew was smiling. 'This is a neat change from pulling people off roofs,' the guy said.

'I'd like Skye to be taken to Whale Head,' Rob told them. 'There was a bit of intervention and I'd like her checked by an obstetrician.'

'Sure thing, Doc. We'll get them to Will-hua, and South Sydney Air can take them on to Whale Head. There won't be any complaints from Douglas. As long as he has his family safe, nothing else matters.'

And as Rob turned and headed into Skye's bedroom to wake her and ready her for the move—Jen had squeaked when she'd heard the boat and was already frantically dressing—those words resonated.

As long as he has his family safe...

More than one family had been formed last night, he thought. Douglas and Skye and their infant daughter. He and Jenny and Jacob.

His family.

Awful things happened—who knew that better than him?—but they were as safe as he could make them. Yes, he was taking a risk moving in with Jen. Lois and Paul's distress would need to be faced head-on, but he and Jen and Jacob would be together, no matter what.

And today... Today the sun was shining. Jen, dressed and ready, was back beside him, giving him a swift hug before she went to wake Skye.

And for a moment Rob turned again and looked at the sun streaming through the window.

The sun was out.

It was time to move on.

CHAPTER FOURTEEN

EMMA'S FUNERAL TOOK place eighteen months later, on a cold winter's day, but with the sun breaking through the clouds enough to make the damp grass in the little Willhua cemetery glisten. There'd been a rainbow intermittently appearing and disappearing during the morning, and as the small entourage gathered around the graveside it emerged again, casting an almost halo-like effect over the scene.

It had been time. No matter what the intervention, the human body had limits. Treating recurring pneumonia had been a constant struggle during these last appalling years, and in the end there'd been no choice. With Rob by her side, with Lois and Paul fighting to the last, she'd slipped away.

And now, finally, they could say goodbye.

With Emma's death, powers of attorney, legal and medical, no longer held sway so the decisions were now Rob's. 'I'd like her buried at

Willhua,' he'd told Lois and Paul, and the couple were too devastated to fight for an alternative, even if they had one. For years they'd refused to face reality and now they had no choice.

But they'd come this morning, for the simple ceremony in the small church out on the headland. And when they'd arrived they'd hugged Jacob—and they'd also hugged Rob. Small beginnings for the future?

On the other side of the grave stood Rob and Jacob—and Jenny. A family. Not legally married, but married in every other sense. Jacob stood between them, a hand in each of theirs. At nearly six he could almost understand what was happening. Paul and Lois had been shocked at the thought of him attending, but Rob had been adamant.

'He's been with Emma every step of this journey. I think he's understood the concept of death more than any child of his age, and he needs to be with us now.'

Us.

Jen gripped Jacob's hand tighter as the coffin was lowered into the open grave. It was close enough to springtime for the wattle to be out everywhere, and they'd organised great sheaths of the soft yellow blooms to be at the graveside. They'd lain wattle on the base of the grave, and as the coffin lowered, wattle was set on top.

The grave could be covered properly later, when Jacob wasn't close. For now all he saw was Emma's coffin being lowered into a cloud of gold.

A final prayer and it was done. Rob lifted his little son and hugged him, and it was time to move on.

But Jen was watching the couple on the far side of the grave, watching their pain, watching the loss they'd never allowed to hit until now. And she touched Rob's arm lightly, she glanced at him, their eyes meeting in a silent message, and then she stepped around the grave to meet them.

'Lois, Paul, I'm so, so sorry,' she said. These were the most prosaic of words, said over and over to all sorts of people, in all sorts of situations. They could hardly make a difference, but they needed to be said.

'I suppose you'll get married now.' That was Lois, and there was such distress behind the words that Jen flinched. But she'd come to talk to them for a purpose and she had to continue.

'Rob and I have already made our vows,' she said, simply but calmly. 'We're already a family. But Emma's still Jacob's mother, and she still feels part of our family. And you're his grandparents and you could be too.'

'You don't want us.'

'We don't want your control,' Jen said gently. 'But we don't want Jacob to lose more than he already has. Rob and I have talked about it. It's early days yet, but whatever happens in the future, anger has no place. Love, though… If you think love for Jacob could let you move forward, Rob and I will be with you every step of the way.'

'We can't…' It was practically a moan from Lois.

'You can't keep loving?' And it was Rob, moving to stand beside her. He was still holding Jacob, cradling the little boy as if he was still a toddler.

But then Jacob wriggled—he'd seen someone he knew. Frankie! Auntie Frankie! Jacob's wriggle was demanding, and Rob lowered him. They all watched as the little boy weaved through the group of the locals who'd supported them so strongly over these last months and found the woman he'd learned to love. Frankie and her crew had even let him go and see her helicopter and sit in the pilot's seat. How awesome an aunt was she?

Frankie knelt and high-fived the little boy and waved to them that she had him in charge. Auntie Frankie. A loved part of Jen's life.

Jen waved back—and then she turned back to Lois and Paul.

You can't keep loving?

That was the question Rob had asked, and it hung, unanswered.

'It just takes courage,' Rob said simply. 'For all of us.'

Then there was a whoop from Jacob and they all turned to see.

'Auntie Frankie has Bruce here!' Jacob yelled. 'Bruce! He's tied up under that tree. She says we'll take him and Stumpy to the park later and Ruth says Bosun can come too. Can we, Jen? Can we, Dad?'

'I don't see why not,' Rob called back. And then he kissed Jen because he needed to. 'It's time to leave,' he said, smiling down at her. 'Em will always be in our hearts, but she'd be the first one to say it's time for us all to move on. Together.'

A birth. A baby. A tiny girl, Stephanie Emma Francesca—because how could Frankie be left out of the equation?

Rob had been with Jen all this long night of labour. Cathy and Angus had been the medics. Rob had simply been…the dad. He was tired now, exhausted beyond belief, but there was no space yet in his life for sleep. He was perched on Jen's bedside, cradling his daughter, gazing down at this new little person and feeling as if his heart might burst.

His daughter.

Jacob had been in to inspect his new sister, but Minnie and the promise of a walk to the playground with Stumpy held much more attraction than a mere baby. Minnie had whisked him away. The medical bustle of birth and aftercare had faded and Rob was left with his wife.

His Jen.

His love.

Love… It was all around them. He could feel it in spades. It was in the way Jen was watching him, the way she was watching her daughter in his arms, the way she was blinking back tears of happiness.

It was also in the way this entire hospital, this entire community was erupting with happiness at the news. Already a small mountain of flowers and soft toys were being left at Reception. He'd seen them in the moments when he'd had to duck out to make fast phone calls after delivery—one to Frankie—of course—one to Jen's parents, who'd answered by satellite phone from somewhere in the Himalayas—and one also to Lois and Paul, who'd responded with delight and a suggestion, tentative, almost humble, that they might meet this new addition to their family.

That could happen, he thought—their relationship had softened to the point where they'd even be welcome. But not today. Today was theirs; it belonged to Jen and Rob.

But they both knew they were surrounded by the care of those who loved them.

He'd brought two of the offerings from Reception back to Jen. One was a tiny, fluffy teddy with a note attached. It was from Anna, mother now of a chubby two-year-old. She was enrolled at online university and sharing her life with her small son and his adoring grandparents. Her note read simply—'*Thank you for my miracle, welcome to yours*'.

The other was from Skye and Douglas—a bunch of wildflowers, with a note which pretty much read the same.

He'd shown the notes to Jen. She'd blinked back more tears and then folded into his arms, their tiny daughter cradled between them.

This was his miracle, he thought. His own private miracle.

And then he thought—what was he thinking? This wasn't private at all.

Jen. Jacob. Minnie. Angus and Cathy. Frankie. Gary. Paul and Lois. The whole community of Willhua.

Love encompassed them all, he thought as he held his wife close. It filled his heart.

'I love you so much,' he whispered.

'Not as much as I love you,' she managed back. 'Oh, Rob, can I be any happier?'

'Let's work on it,' he told her, kissing her hair and then tilting her chin to kiss her lips. And then, as the kiss finally ended…

'Let's take it as our personal challenge,' he whispered. 'You and me and our family and our community—even our dogs. Take fair warning, my own sweet love. Happy-ever-after, here we come.'

* * * * *

Look out for the next story in the
Paramedics and Pups duet

The Italian, His Pup and Me
by Alison Roberts

And if you enjoyed this story, check
out these other great reads from
Marion Lennox

Healed by Their Dolphin Island Baby
Dr. Finlay's Courageous Bride
A Family to Save the Doctor's Heart

All available now!